Dangerous Splendor

DANGEROUS SPLENDOR

Lucy Fuchs

AVALON BOOKS

THOMAS BOUREGY AND COMPANY, INC.
22 EAST 60TH STREET • NEW YORK 10022

PRINTED IN THE UNITED STATES OF AMERICA
BY THE BOOK PRESS, BRATTLEBORO, VERMONT

This is for Frank, my husband,
with much love

CHAPTER I

I had my first glimpse of Ayers Rock at sunset. I shall never forget that first impression. Even after all the strange experiences I had later at the mountain, that first view of it, glowing with the setting sun, will be forever a powerful memory.

We, the passengers of the bus, had just traveled 300 miles from Alice Springs in the heart of Australia. The last 150 miles of road were not paved at all, but nobody complained. We were all on our way to see the rock. Most of the rest were tourists, I surmised, with cameras around their necks and guidebooks on Australia.

I, with my portfolio carefully stowed in the baggage compartment and with my valise full of paints, was not a tourist. I liked to think of myself as an artist. But I had never sold a painting. Not even my teacher at the Art Institute really thought I was an artist. Yet.

But my mother saw me as a real artist. Each day after class when I hurried home she would be waiting for me, propped up in her bed. Before I could even ask how she was she wanted to see my work. Always she would look at it carefully, her face serious and appreciative.

"Melissa," she would say, "this is good. I can see you are making progress. You are the painter that I had hoped one day to be." She made no attempt to pretend that she thought she was getting better.

"I am not going to live long," she told me often, "and before I die I want you to be on your way to being an established artist."

I lost the race against time. The day came when she was in too much pain to ask about my painting. I rushed her to the hospital. There her condition deteriorated rapidly, and she died within a few days.

"In a certain sense she was lucky," her doctor had said. "I have seen others like your mother suffer from cancer for months in excruciating pain."

His words soothed my own pain a little.

The light on the rock also helped to soothe my pain. For I was in Australia because it had been my mother's wish.

She had not made a will. "There is no money," she had said, "and you are all I have in the world. But there will be some insurance money, Melissa. And I want you to promise me that you will use it to go to Australia to paint Ayers Rock. Ayers Rock is the most vivid impression I have of my wedding trip. I want you to have a chance to see it."

She paused and breathed deeply, and I knew how painful each breath was to her.

"Melissa, promise me that you will go to Ayers Rock and paint it," she had said. "I feel sure that you will find your inspiration there. Promise me."

And so now I was there, standing outside the bus looking at the rock.

How strange it was, a huge flattened leaf of a mountain, standing all alone on the parched and wild heartland of Australia. The setting sun lit up the rock with a deep red glow that seemed to take fire from within.

And then, suddenly, the sun slipped behind the edge of the world and it was dark. A chill came up suddenly.

I wandered slowly back to the bus with the others.

"All aboard," Dennis, the bus driver, said. "We will now go over to the hotel. I want to warn you, this hotel is adequate, but it is not classified as luxurious. However, I am sure that you will not be too critical when you remember the distance from Alice Springs and the problem of transporting materials here."

It was only a short drive over to the hotel, the best of the three that were in the area. It was a low, flat building with wings going out in all directions like an octopus.

Dennis helped the receptionist. "Room sixty-two, Miss Carrington," he said, giving me my key.

I lugged my portfolio and valise around to the back of the hotel to find Room sixty-two.

"Here, let me help you," a young male American voice said.

I turned to see who it was and caught my breath. Walking right behind me was the most handsome man I had ever seen. He was tall and lanky with blond wavy hair and blue eyes that sparkled with excitement.

"Hello, lovely lady," he said, smiling. "I am Larry O'Brien. And I'd be honored to help you carry your luggage."

"All right," I said. "Yes. Thank you."

"And your name, Mademoiselle?" he asked.

"I am Melissa Carrington," I said, "from Chicago."

"And what are you doing here in Australia, little girl? So far from home?" He paused and then went on.

"Wait, let me guess. You came here to paint?" He was looking at my portfolio.

"Right," I said. "What about you?"

"I came to explore," he said. "I'm an explorer, an adventurer."

We rounded the building just then. "What is your number?" he asked.

"Sixty-two," I said. "It should be around here."

"Here it is, fair lady," Larry said, putting the key in the lock. He pushed open the door and switched on the light.

The bus driver had been right. In no sense of the word could the room be called luxurious. The naked bulb from the ceiling gave the only light on the twin beds and a small dresser. There were two small chairs and in the corner was a very small bathroom.

I turned on the water at the sink. It coughed and sputtered but water came. "Well, at least there's running water," I said.

"And that's about all," Larry said. "Look, let's get a drink before dinner. You look like you could use some refreshment."

I hesitated. "Well, all right," I said, "but give me a little time. I need a chance to freshen up."

Larry smiled and said good-naturedly, "OK, I'll meet you at the bar in a little while. All right?"

"Right," I said, "and thank you for helping me with my luggage."

When he left, I washed up and did a little unpacking. What would be appropriate to wear to a bar in the Outback of Australia?

At last I chose a simple white pantsuit and decided to put my hair down. All day I had had my long black hair wound up tightly around my head. Now I brushed it and let it fall over my shoulders.

"Your hair is your best feature," my mother had said. "Take good care of it. It brings out the lights in your dark eyes."

I smiled to myself, thinking about my mother. She would have liked Larry. She never said much, but I knew she would have wanted me to date more than I did. I don't have time for dates, I said to myself, I want to be an artist. All I've ever wanted to do was paint.

And what about Larry? We shall see.

I left my room and carefully locked it behind me. My clothes weren't worth much, but my paints were quite expensive. It suddenly dawned on me how difficult it would be to get paints out here.

I wandered over to the bar and looked in. There was nothing fancy about it either. And Larry wasn't there.

I stepped outside, somewhat surprised and cha-grined. Well, I had no intention of drinking alone.

I heard voices around the corner and moved in the direction of the noise. There under a dim light sat an old woman in a wheelchair. Around her a group of people were gathered. I could see Larry's blond head among them. He looked up and saw me.

"Melissa," he said, "come here. You must meet Catherine."

"Who is this Catherine?" I asked.

"She's blind," Larry said, "and she lives here at Ayers Rock all the time. She loves this place because, according to her, this is the most sacred spot on earth."

A man standing near us added, "She is blind, but she can see people's minds. They say she can tell the future too."

I looked at Catherine, her white hair surrounding her head like a halo under the light. Her face was lined and wrinkled but there was a softness and a radiance about it. Just then she was holding the hand of a middle-aged woman.

"You are a tourist, aren't you?" she asked the woman, who nodded vigorously. "You came here to see Ayers Rock. You will have a good time here," she said, "but don't climb it. It will be too difficult for you."

Larry looked at me. "That's no great prophecy," he whispered. "I could have told her that."

The plump woman went away satisfied.

Catherine spoke softly. "Is there a young woman here in the crowd?" she asked. "An American?"

Larry looked at me with a smile. "I guess that's you," he said. "Go on."

I held back, but others in the crowd had heard Larry.

"Go ahead," the man near me urged. "Catherine may have something interesting to tell you."

Reluctantly I went up to Catherine.

"You are the young American," she said. "Let me take your hand."

She held my hand in her soft yet firm hand for what seemed like a long time. Then she whispered, in a barely audible voice. "You came to Ayers Rock," she said, "to find something. You may find it. I hope you do, for if you do not, you will leave more unhappy than ever. *If* you leave at all. I see great danger here for you."

She looked at me then, although I knew she could not see me.

"Young American," she said, "please be careful, be very careful!"

CHAPTER II

Larry was smiling. "Don't let that dear old lady bother you," he said. "She's an entertainer. She knows her audience wants to be frightened a little."

I smiled, but I was really rather shaken. "How does she support herself?" I asked.

"I don't know," Larry said. "Maybe she's rich. Some people are lucky. But enough of that. Look, we've got time for a drink before dinner. Come on." He propelled me, without further ado, into the bar and ordered drinks.

"So you're going to try to paint Ayers Rock," he said. "That sounds interesting. Me, I want to climb the north side. I've climbed the tourist side before."

"Is that dangerous?"

Larry laughed, showing his white teeth. "Only if you're out of shape. This isn't real mountain climbing, you know, with hooks and ropes. This is just pulling yourself up step by step. Strictly amateur stuff. Actually it's easy."

"Easy for you," I said. "You like to try things."

"Yes," he said, "I believe in trying everything at least once."

The Rock Hotel had a dinner hour for its guests and it soon became clear that that was the only time dinner was served. There wasn't even a choice of meals.

"Just like a prison dining room," Larry said, as we entered.

"Not really," I said with a laugh. "At least we have a choice about whom we want to eat with."

Larry chose a table for us near the corner where three teenage girls were sitting. The waitress started to serve even though the sixth seat remained empty. Larry was interested in the teenagers.

"And what is your name?" he asked one of the girls.

"Doreen," said the red-headed girl.

"I've always loved redheads," he said. Then he turned to the other two, both blondes. "Not that I don't like blondes. In fact, I love blondes."

The two girls giggled.

"I'm Sylvia," one said, and the other said in a lilting tone: "My name is Georgia. I'll never forgive my parents for naming me that."

"Why not?" Larry asked. "It's a lovely name."

"Is this seat taken?" asked a voice near me.

I looked up to see a mustached, brown-haired man.

"No, please sit down," I told him. Larry glanced at him and turned back to the girls.

"Here, have some roast beef," I said to the new-comer. "Looks like it is family style here."

"Ah, yes," he said, then introduced himself. "I'm Frank Hanson."

"And I am Melissa Carrington. This is Larry O'Brien, and the girls are Doreen, Sylvia, and Georgia."

They barely looked up as I said their names.

Frank looked at me. "Let me see, you're American too, aren't you?"

"Yes," I said, "like you. But are you a tourist? You don't look exactly like one."

Frank chuckled softly. "That word tourist is bad, isn't it? But places like this need tourists, I guess. If they didn't have them, there would be fewer conveniences for people like me."

"And what do you do?"

"I'm an anthropologist. I study people. I'm especially interested in studying the aborigines. This is a good place for them, you know."

"So I've heard."

"And what about you?" Frank asked.

"She's a painter," Larry interjected.

"A painter!" Frank nodded approvingly. "I've often thought that Ayers Rock would be an excellent subject. But difficult to capture."

"Well," I said, "I just arrived. Tomorrow I plan to set up my easel and see what I can do. I've only seen the rock once and there seem to be mysteries at the heart of it."

"There are indeed," Frank said, and then he fell silent. He was polite during the rest of the meal, but he seemed preoccupied.

After dinner Larry suggested that we all take an evening walk over to the rock. Frank politely declined. The girls agreed, boisterously happy at the idea.

"You go ahead," I said. "I think I'll get some sleep, so I'll be ready to paint tomorrow."

Larry smiled at me. "Oh, come on, lovely lady."

But I shook my head and went to my room. I could hear the girls giggling as they left.

In my room I faced up to my feelings. I was angry with Larry. He invited me to dinner and then practically ignored me. Well, that was enough of him!

I thought about Catherine and felt afraid. But I straightened my shoulders and brushed my fears aside. After all, how could I get hurt just looking at the rock?

I already regretted not going to the rock with Larry and the girls. I was lonely in my barren room, so I decided to wander around the hotel. There were not many people outside. Of course not, I realized. There's no swimming pool, no grass. It's not much more than a barren parking lot.

I walked past the bar. There were a few people there, but they all seemed engrossed in their conversations. Then I saw a sign. Slides of Ayers Rock were being shown in the recreation room.

Well, watching slides was better than being alone. Besides, the slides might give me some ideas of the rock.

An old man was already showing the slides to a handful of people when I went in. I slipped into the nearest chair. To my surprise and amazement, the slides were beautiful.

There were slides of the rock at sunrise when it shone with a yellow glow. In others, in the evening, the rock looked crimson red or deep violet. Some slides were taken at night, by the light of the moon, and they showed a looming hulk of blackness. Two slides showed a golden rock topped with a rainbow. When the show was over and the people had filed out, I wandered over to the old man.

"Those are beautiful slides," I said. "Are they yours?"

"Yes," he said. "I go out about every day. Those represent the best of about twenty years."

"Twenty years!" I exclaimed. "You mean you've been here that long?"

"I just can't seem to get away," he said. "I came to see the rock and spend a few weeks on a temporary job. And now I find I can't leave. That rock holds me."

"Well," I said, "I am very pleased to meet you. I'll be staying here a few weeks, trying to paint the rock. You may be able to help me get some insights. My name is Melissa Carrington."

"I am Colin Ledger." The old man shook my hand roughly. "I shall be pleased to help you in any way I can. You can always find me. I'm around most of the time. When I'm not taking pictures, I'm carrying luggage, or repairing motors or tires. There's plenty for a general handyman to do around here."

We talked a while then about the rock. He told me some of the legends of the Carpent Snake people who long ago inhabited the rock, their fights with alien tribes, their mysterious rites.

"The aborigines believe themselves to be descended from those people of long ago," he said. "The rock was, and still is, sacred to them. You know, there are parts of the rock where no one ever goes—no one white, that is. Out of respect for aborigine custom, we don't enter their sacred areas."

"They still carry on their customs?" I asked.

"Yes," said Colin, "but only on very special occasions. Their customs are almost forgotten by many of their young men..."

Suddenly I realized that it was getting late.

"Well, thank you very much," I said to Colin. "I hope to see you again soon."

I hurried back to my room, tired now. But I had only gone a few feet when I saw Doreen, Sylvia, and Georgia.

"Hello," Sylvia said, giggling.

"How was the rock?" I asked.

"The rock was lovely," said Doreen, "but Larry got away."

They scampered off. I smiled to myself. So Larry got away from them too, I thought. So much for Larry. I'll take Colin any day.

As I walked back toward my room, I thought about the next day. The bus would take people to the rock to see the sunrise. I could get up even earlier and walk over.

I decided to set my alarm and try for the bus.

I went down the darkened passageways outside to find my room. Sixty-two, where was it? I seemed to be in the right area, but where was sixty-two? Something wasn't right. I squinted at the numbers on the doors. Eighty-two! I was two branches over. The octopus arms had confused me.

Suddenly I heard a familiar voice. It was coming from a room I was approaching.

The door stood half open and Larry's blond hair shone in the room's light. I did not turn and look directly, but from what I saw as I passed, he seemed to be talking to a dark-haired man.

"Give me time," Larry was saying. "I'll get them to you. It's just a matter of finding the right time."

"You'd better hurry." The man's voice was rough, though quiet. "I'm leaving in a few days and when I go, I take them with me."

At this I heard Larry laugh. "Yes, but you'll leave some goodies with me too," he said.

He said more, but I was out of earshot.

What was all that about? I wondered, as I found my room. Whatever it was, it was none of my business!

And then I resolutely bathed and got ready for bed.

I did not sleep well that night. I dreamed of blind Catherine holding my hand and warning me over and over, "Leave Ayers Rock, leave Ayers Rock!"

CHAPTER III

I awoke with a start when my alarm rang. It was pitch dark. I hadn't slept enough. My stomach was begging for a cup of coffee.

You might as well be quiet, I said to my stomach. You know the dining room won't be open until eight. By then, we will have seen the sunrise.

It didn't take me long to dress in the chilly morning, and then I hurried to the bus. It was already half full of other half-asleep people.

Nobody said much. Everyone just sort of pulled his coat around him and huddled in his seat.

Then I heard a familiar voice behind me. "Hello, Melissa."

I turned. It was Frank. He smiled warmly at me. "How are you today?" he asked.

"Fine, thank you," I said. "And you?"

"Well," he said, "good enough at least to get up before dawn to see a rock!"

He laughed softly and I felt warmed.

The bus pulled out, screeching noisily. Quiet exag-

14

gerates sound I remembered. I turned back to Frank, but he had his eyes closed. Trying to catch up on sleep, I thought. Good idea.

But I did not close my eyes. I came halfway around the world, I thought, to see a rock. And I was not about to miss a bit of it.

There was just a little light from the east as the bus pulled onto an open space near the rock. I took up a spot where I could get full view of the rock, unimpeded by anything.

I glanced around for Frank. He was standing near the bus, but he seemed to be studying the tourists, not the rock.

And then slowly, the sun peeked up from the edge of the world. It seemed to flirt with the few low-lying clouds around it. And then, even as we watched, it slipped up from behind them and focused directly on the rock.

The transformation was amazing. The rock, which had seemed dark gray a minute before, suddenly burst into flame, warm and inviting. It was alive.

I felt completely drawn to it. Cameras were clicking all around me, but I hardly noticed.

Suddenly the glow was gone. The sun was no longer reserving its light just for the rock. It spread the light all over the bare ground, the scrubby bushes...

The effect was ruined.

Now, as we boarded the bus again, everyone was in a good mood. It was as if the rock had warmed up everyone with its glow.

"So the rock has captured you," Frank said, joining me in the seat.

"Yes, I guess so," I said. "What about you?"

"Me," he said, "I love the rock. But I try to see it as

the aborigines did. They were much less interested in the beauty of the rock than its sacredness. It was like a mother to them, a source of food and life."

"Will you be talking to aborigines today?" I asked.

"I hope to," said Frank. "I learned their language in Alice Springs and I want to learn all I can here."

We were back at the hotel by then and everyone trooped into the dining room. Everyone but Frank. He excused himself, said, "See you later," and was gone.

I was joined by Doreen, Sylvia, and Georgia as I entered the room.

"Hello," Sylvia said. "We're going to climb the rock today."

They were anxious to have an audience. Well, I thought, I'll oblige. But what was it about their youth that made me feel so old? I was only twenty-three myself!

"Well," I said, "so you three are going to climb the rock. The tourist side?"

"Yes, I guess so," said Georgia, "for a start."

"Larry told us that he is going to try the north side," Doreen said. "After we do the tourist climb, maybe we'll try the north side too."

"Is it dangerous?" I asked. "Larry seemed to think it is a little more risky."

Sylvia leaned forward conspiratorially. "I heard that a man fell off the rock at the north end last year," she said. "He was actually blown off."

"The winds are very strong out there, Larry said."

"Where is Larry?" asked Georgia. All three girls looked at me hopefully.

"I don't know," I said. "I didn't see him on the bus this morning."

The girls looked disappointed. They lost interest in me and started to look around the dining room. But Larry did not appear.

They were off for the climb right after breakfast. I went to collect my easel and my paints, then I made my way over to the rock.

By now full daylight had come and I had a better chance to see the stark brutality of the land. It was not really a desert the way I had always pictured it. To me a desert always seemed to be shifting dunes of sand.

This land was entirely covered with a low scrubby bush called spinifex, or porcupine grass. There were even a few small trees. But nowhere was the land good enough for grain farming or even for raising cattle. Instead, as the aborigines learned long ago, if you watched and waited carefully, you could find a few small animals to kill to eat.

And you could find water at the rock. That was the big attraction there. When it rains, and it does rain occasionally, water runs off the rock in huge amounts. It collects at little life-giving pools like Maggie Springs.

I set up my easel near the rock, trying to see it in a different light. Maybe in the few weeks that I would be here, I would have a chance to paint the rock from all angles.

This morning I was facing west, trying to catch the rock in the full light of the morning sun. I couldn't quite get a good perspective. Maybe if I moved my easel a little closer . . .

I tried that and looked again. Something wasn't right. The rock just stood there. It was not alive. And I knew that if I painted it like that, it would be the way my professor at the Art Institute had labeled my work: "Not alive!"

But I had to get started. I filled my brush with blue and started to work in the sky. At least I knew I could handle that.

Once I had the sky in, I stopped. This just isn't going to work, I thought. I need some way to get to know the rock.

I approached it. I was on a side that was not visited too much. The three girls would be climbing the tourist side, and the north side.

But Larry must have changed his mind. For there he was, climbing up the side nearest me, slowly and painstakingly pulling himself up the rock. He did not see me at first.

I held my breath, watching the perilous climb. Then he turned and saw me. His face registered surprise. Then he smiled and began to descend.

I watched him, frightened that he might slip down the mountain. "Be careful," I shouted. "Be careful."

He jumped down to the ground and came over to me, flashing a warm smile.

"Well, it's Miss Melissa," he said. "And I do think she cares about me! Were you afraid that I was going to fall?"

"Well, it looked pretty scary," I said. "But why did you quit climbing? Does an audience bother you?"

Larry smiled again. "No," he said, "I love an audience. But I decided I would rather be with you than watched by you."

He took my arm then. "I'll show you around," he said, and he walked me around to a little cave nearby.

"This cave," he said, "used to be a waiting cave. I understand that the women used to wait here while their young men were being initiated into their puberty rites. Those rites were quite painful. They used to smear blood on the walls of the cave, which is next door. But you can't see it because it's reserved."

It was rather dark in the little waiting cave. Larry urged me in. He pulled out a small flashlight and shone it around.

"I see you came prepared," I said.

"Yes, that's me," he said. "The eagle scout, always ready."

"Were you really an eagle scout?" I asked.

"I, my dear lady, was all kinds of things. Still am, including a playboy."

He leaned over and planted a solid kiss on my lips.

I moved out of the cave. "Larry," I said, "you don't have to demonstrate. I believe you." I started on around the rock and came to a wire fence.

"Don't go that way," Larry said. "That's the aborigine compound."

"That must be the sacred place," I said.

"Yes," said Larry. And then he shouted, "Look out!"

He gave me a shove away from the mountain, and I fell down, stunned, as a huge rock crashed down just where I had been standing.

CHAPTER IV

"Larry," I said, "I could have been killed!"

"Yes," he said thoughtfully. "Look up there. It must have worked itself loose."

I looked up the nearly straight side of the mountain. Yes, it was possible. It was also terribly frightening.

"Larry," I said, "thank you for pushing me away. You saved my life."

"Well," he said, "it was just lucky that I saw it coming. It would be a pity for a pretty girl like you to get hurt."

He paused, and then he added, "All the same, it's interesting. I wonder if that's what Catherine meant."

Catherine! She had said that my life would be in danger.

"You don't believe in her, do you?" I asked. "I thought you had pooh-poohed her ideas."

"So I did," said Larry, "but maybe I was wrong. Maybe you should get away from here."

I laughed shakily. "Well," I said, "I'll get away from the mountain for a while. I want to get back to my paints."

Just then I heard a giggle and I knew immediately who it was.

Doreen led the way as usual. "Here's our Larry," she called out. "Larry, where have you been? Come and climb with us."

Larry looked at me in mock surrender. "Looks like I'm captured," he said. "Well, see you later, lovely lady." Then he added more softly, "Listen, think about what we talked about, will you?"

Georgia flashed me a look that seemed distinctly jealous. I chuckled to myself.

I didn't come here to be scared away that easily. I had made a promise to my mother and I was going to stick by it. But right now I had no desire to stand so close to the rock. I looked at it, trying to capture some of its size. Five miles around a rock that was all of one material, the largest monolith in the world, the guide-book said.

Suddenly I saw a glint of light on a small pebble at the base of the rock, right near where Larry and I had been standing.

Curious, I went over to pick it up. It was a dullish gray color, but it didn't seem to be like the rock.

Well, it was rather interesting. Later today I would ask Colin Ledger about it. Now I would get back to my painting. I found my canvas still there, the cloudless, brilliant blue sky now dry. And now I was able to start on the rock. I began with the sheer side I had just visited. It took a long time, as I worked hard to capture the grays, the reds, and the vermillion.

I was deeply engrossed in my work when a shadow fell across my canvas. I turned quickly and recognized the dark-haired man who had been talking to Larry last night.

"This is good work," he said, barely smiling.

"Thank you," I said.

"I'm pleased to meet an artist," he said, extending his hand. "I am Ralph Thompson."

"And I am Melissa Carrington," I said. "I hope to be an artist, but I don't consider myself one yet."

"You are getting there," he said seriously.

"What about you?" I asked. "Are you a tourist?"

"Yes." he said, "I'm an Australian tourist. From Melbourne.You're so young and you've come all the way from America to see the rock. I live right here in this country but it has taken me forty-three years to get here."

"Don't feel bad," I said. "There are many places in the United States I haven't seen yet."

He smiled then and asked, "Have you seen Larry O'Brien today? Was he over here earlier?" Then he added, "Larry and I are old friends. Or rather I am a friend of his father."

I hesitated. There was something about this man that made me nervous. "Well," I said at last, "when I saw him, he was going off with three girls. I think they were going to climb the rock."

"Ah," he said. "Well, thank you very much."

He left then, but not without first going up to the rock and scanning it carefully. I watched as he approached the fence that surrounded the aborigine compound. Then he sauntered off, with studied casualness.

I decided that I was hungry. I had done quite enough for one morning. And, remembering the rock that had almost smashed me, I had had quite enough scares.

The sun was warm by now too. I packed up my paints and easel and headed back to the hotel.

The place was buzzing. A busload of tourists had just arrived and they were getting their keys from their rooms.

Catherine was sitting in a darkened corner. Her face had the expression of one who watches and waits. On an impulse I went up to her. As I approached her chair, her facial expression changed.

"Come here, child," she said in her soft, melodious voice. "Come here. I want to hear how your morning went."

She reached out and took my hand. "You've had a bad scare this morning," she said. "It is not the last!"

I had not even spoken to her. Had she recognized my footsteps?

"Catherine," I said, "how did you know it was me, and how did you know what had happened this morning?"

"I know, Melissa," she said. "There are many things that one sees, but not with the eyes."

"Catherine," I said, quite intrigued now, "what do you mean, it is not the last?"

She looked at me directly, with unseeing eyes. "Melissa," she said, "take my advice and be very careful. I see some very frightening things happening. And yet..."

"What?" I asked.

Catherine shook her head. "There is much more to tell you," she said, "but I cannot tell you now."

I wanted to ask more, but already tourists were coming up to Catherine, anxious to visit her.

Back in my room, I breathed a sigh of relief. It was good to get back. I showered and immediately felt better. Then I left to go to the dining room.

It was full of the new tourists, the packaged-tour kind who would be spending the afternoon and evening here and would be gone late tomorrow.

"It's a long trip for such a short time," said one of the elderly women who sat down by me.

"Yes, it certainly is," I said. "It seems like you need more time than that to see the rock."

"Yes," said the other woman, "but if we stayed here much longer we wouldn't have time to see the opal mines at Coober Pedy. As it is, we'll have to catch our plane within just a few hours when we get back to Alice Springs."

They talked on and on of their two-week whirlwind tour of Australia.

They were smothering me. As soon as I finished my meal I hurried outside to breathe the open air and look at the rock.

Then I remembered the odd piece of rock I had found that morning. Maybe I could find Colin and ask about it.

I went to my room to get it. As I rounded the corner to my wing, I almost crashed into Frank Hanson. He stopped and said, "Well, hello, Melissa. Did you have a pleasant morning?"

"Yes," I said. "I started a painting today. And I even made a little progress."

"That's good," he said. "Maybe sometime you'll let me see it."

"All right," I said, "but not until it's finished."

"Fine," he said.

I felt a little puzzled by him. His attitude was warm and friendly on the surface, but there was an aloofness about him. It was as if he was always preoccupied.

I got to my room and put the key in the lock.

Strange, it wasn't locked. Had I neglected to lock it before lunch? Or was it the maid? Had someone come in to clean? I doubted that, since the bed had been made already when I was here before lunch.

Perhaps it was just my carelessness. But I knew that I was never careless about locking my door.

I took a quick look around the room. Well, I thought, everything seems to be just as it was. Let's see, what did I come to get? The stone. I had slipped it into the zippered pocket of my jacket this morning.

I felt in the zippered pocket. It was not there. I checked the other pocket. Empty.

Did it drop on the floor? No, there was nothing on the floor.

I was puzzled now, but not really disturbed. After all, it could have dropped out when I came in. Could it? Do things fall out of zippered pockets?

Or was I mistaken? Did I actually put it somewhere else? Perhaps I had put it among my paints. I decided to check them, although I knew it was not likely. When I had finished painting this morning I had cleaned my brushes and put everything together neatly.

I went over to check the satchel I carried my paints in when I worked outside. As soon as I lifted it, I felt a cold chill. One of the paint brushes was lying on the floor, near the bag.

I knew it had dropped out, but I had not left it like that. Someone had rummaged through my things. Someone had been looking for something. What?

Quickly, I pulled out my suitcase, looked through everything. Nothing seemed to be missing.

I looked around the room. My only valuables were my paints and equipment, but they were valuable only to me. And they were all there.

My money, in travelers' checks, was in my purse and I had carried my purse to the dining room with me.

There was only one thing missing: the strange and ugly stone I had found at the rock. What would some-one want that for?

Well, there was one man who would probably know something about it: Colin Ledger.

CHAPTER V

Colin was leaning against the hotel, near the entrance. He smiled warmly when he saw me. "Hello, Melissa. It's nice to see you. Did you do some painting this morning?"

"Yes," I said, "a little. Colin, do you have a minute? I'd like to talk to you."

He looked at me carefully. "My, but you look serious," he said. "Yes, let's talk. I think that the new batch of tourists are pretty well settled. Can I buy you a beer in the bar? That way, people will be able to find me if they need me. Will that be all right?"

"Yes, fine," I said.

The bar was cool and nearly empty. We sat at a small table and Colin said, "Now, tell me what I can do for you."

"Well," I said, "this morning I painted the west side of the rock. I stayed at a distance from it to paint but later I went closer. Two strange things happened. A large rock fell and almost hit me. You know Larry O'Brien, don't you?"

Colin nodded.

"Well, he was there and he pushed me aside just in time. I might have been killed!"

Colin looked at me very seriously. "That is very strange," he said. "Very seldom do rocks just slide down. Although, of course, it is quite possible. I'm very glad you weren't hurt. I want to explore that a little later. What was the second strange thing?"

"Afterwards I found a strange little rock, just an unusual stone, I thought. I brought it home. I was sure I put it in my zippered pocket. But it's not there now."

"Wait," said Colin. "Did you show this stone to Larry?"

"No," I said, "I found it after Larry had left."

"Go on," Colin said. "Did you lose it, perhaps?"

"I don't know how I could have," I said, "but listen. When I got back to my room after lunch, the door wasn't locked. One of my paint brushes was out of my satchel. I know I didn't leave one out. Someone came in my room during lunch and took the pebble."

"Hmm," Colin murmured, sipping his beer.

"You don't think I'm imagining things, do you?"

"No," Colin said thoughtfully. "No, I don't think so. Tell me about that stone. What was its color?"

"Well, it was dull, but it looked very different from the mountain. I was interested in that, because if Ayers Rock is a monolith, the whole thing should be of the same material."

"Yes," said Colin. He sipped his beer. Then he said, "Melissa, I think I'd better tell you something. I don't want to scare you, but I want to put you on guard.

"I'm not sure what the stone was," said Colin. "As a matter of fact, I feel it's probably not even valuable. It only means something to those involved. What I have to tell you is this: About a year ago, a young man was killed at Ayers."

He stopped and looked at me. Then he laughed. "Now, don't start trembling. He fell off the rock. Unfortunately, that happens every so often here. But there seemed to be something strange about his death. He had a number of relatives who came here to see where he died. But they all seemed to be searching for something."

"Colin," I said, "you're making all this very vague and scary."

"I'm not trying to do that," he said. "I just want you to be careful. Don't climb the rock."

"I didn't plan on doing that."

"I know, you're not the climbing type. Tourists climb the rock every day, but still there are too many accidents out there for me to be comfortable about it."

"I heard about the plaques."

"Yes," Colin said softly, "but those three plaques, remembering three persons who fell, do not represent the total number of accidents. Just be careful!"

"Mr. Ledger," the hotel receptionist called, "there is a guest in Room ninety-eight who needs you."

"All right," said Colin, rising. "I guess I've got to go to work."

"Thanks for the beer," I said. "But especially, thanks for your time and advice. Even though I feel uneasy."

"Yes," said Colin. "I'm sorry that I frightened you. Listen, I show my slides every night after supper. Come over and I'll tell you more."

I finished my beer and left. I did feel very uneasy. And then, outside the bar I saw Frank.

"Well, we meet again," he said.

"How are things going?" I asked.

"Well," he said, "just now I was planning to go over to the rock and see one of the caves. Would you like to go with me?"

"Yes, I would," I said, very pleased to have his company.

"All right," he said. "I want to look at the so-called maternity cave."

We walked over to the rock, slowly, keeping time with Frank's gentle voice. He had seen a few aborigines this morning, he told me.

"Did you get a chance to talk to them?" I asked.

"Only briefly," he answered. "Unfortunately, there are too many curious tourists who come with too many foolish questions."

"Like what?"

"Aborigines are always being asked to show their poisoned arrows. Now, there are some aborigines who still know how to make poison for arrows, but they certainly don't do it around here. And they use it only for killing game, like kangeroos."

"Yes," I said. "I can imagine that they must be annoyed with questions like that."

"Well," Frank said seriously, "the aborigines here in Australia are suffering what usually happens to any nontechnical people when they meet the technical world. Incidentally, notice that I call them nontechnical, not primitive. The more you get to know of their life, the more you realize that it was extremely complex.

"But as I was saying, when any nontechnical tribe meets a technical one, the nontechnical one seems to suffer. They usually do not fully accept the technical, but they give up much of the nontechnical knowledge that was passed down through the ages. As a consequence, many members of the tribe find themselves today in a never-never land, living fully in neither world."

"That's very interesting," I said. "It could explain some of the apparent apathy of the aborigines."

"Right," said Frank.

When we reached the rock, Frank led the way to the cave. It was low and very rocky, very uncomfortable.

We entered the cave then and sat down on the low rocks. We were entirely alone.

"It's very quiet in here," I said. "There's a peacefulness. And yet I can imagine women in here suffering the pains of giving birth."

"Yes," said Frank softly. "It's unfortunate that you're not an anthropologist. We could use some more female anthropologists to study women."

"You know," he went on, "these women do not talk easily to foreign men. It's difficult for them even to talk to their husbands, much less to strangers."

I smiled. "It sounds so interesting. But I'm not much of a student. And I couldn't learn the language if I tried. I barely made it through two years of Spanish."

We spent quite a while in the cave. I felt relaxed, comfortable with Frank. But our conversation was quite impersonal. When the sun started to sink low in the west I said, "Looks like we'd better head back."

We walked around to where we could get a better view of the sun on the rock. Just last night I had had my first glimpse of Ayers Rock, I mused. And today I already feel that I know the rock a little better.

"Come, I'll show you a great place to see the rock," Frank said.

We climbed a small mound some distance from the tourist area. Frank was right. The view from there was magnificent.

The sun set slowly and cast its red glow over everything. At the final moment before it disappeared, it hit the rock with full force. The rock shone alone in a dark world.

I held my breath. And then it was gone.

"Beautiful!" I exclaimed.

"Yes," said Frank softly, gently taking my arm. "I never get tired of looking at it. But now let's get back to the hotel."

We walked slowly, picking our way carefully through the low bushes. By the time we reached the hotel, other tourists were crowding around the dining room.

But people were not entering to eat. They were milling around, talking excitedly.

"Something's happened," I said to Frank.

"Yes," he said. "Perhaps there was an accident."

Just then Georgia and I spied each other.

"Melissa!" she exclaimed, running over to me. "Isn't it horrible?"

"What?" I asked. "We just got here."

"Do you know that old caretaker, Colin Ledger?" she asked. "He drowned at Maggie Springs."

CHAPTER VI

"Colin drowned!" I exclaimed.

"Yes," Georgia said. "Isn't it horrible?"

Frank held me closer. "Are you all right?" he asked. "You're trembling!"

"I just talked to Colin this morning," I said. "Just this morning."

"Let's find out more about this," Frank said.

Gradually we got the whole story. Colin had apparently gone off on one of his picture-taking expeditions late this afternoon. No one saw him again until a tourist found his body in Maggie Springs.

"But Maggie Springs isn't very deep," Frank said. "I wouldn't have thought it was deep enough to drown in."

"No," said the receptionist, our informant. "It's quite shallow, except near the base of the rock, where it is pretty deep. And that's where Colin was. He must have lost his footing and slipped and hit his head. His photographic equipment held him down."

"Was there—" I hesitated, then blurted out, "was

there any evidence of foul play?"

The employee stared at me. "No," she said. "Who would want to hurt Colin?" She was close to tears.

Frank and I moved away. But now he was puzzled. "Surely it was an accident," he said.

"Yes," I said simply, not at all convinced.

Eventually the excitement died down and people remembered that they were hungry. Each table buzzed with the news of Colin's death.

Frank sat beside me at the table. He tried in vain to get me to talk, to cheer me up.

"Colin must have meant a lot to you," he said.

"Well," I answered slowly, "I didn't really know him, of course. I talked to him only twice in the time that I've been here. But he made a good impression on me. He seemed to be such a warm and caring human being."

Frank touched my hand. "Yes," he said, "I understand."

After supper Frank asked me whether I wanted to take a walk.

"No," I said, "but thank you. Right now I just want to be alone and to get some sleep."

I went to my room. As soon as I entered, I felt a chill. I closed the door and looked around carefully. Then I checked my painting materials. Things were exactly as I had left them. Then I checked the closet, the drawers. Yes, there they were, all just as I had left them.

I breathed a sigh of relief and went back and locked the door. Then I sat down to think about Colin. I did not for one minute think that his death was an accident. Something was going on around here.

I sat there a long time not wanting to go to bed, but neither did I want to go out and meet people. I stared at my painting of the rock. Tomorrow I would get back to it. But now I felt helpless to do anything.

Then there was a knock on the door. In my gloomy mood I was frightened. I just sat and listened.

The knock came again. And then a voice: "Melissa, are you there? It's Larry."

"Yes," I said. "What do you want?"

"Melissa, can I talk to you a minute? Please."

"All right, Larry," I said reluctantly. I didn't really want to talk to anyone. I unlocked and opened the door. Larry stood there, his blond hair shining.

"Are you lonely, lovely lady?" he asked, grinning and showing his perfect teeth.

"No," I said, somewhat annoyed. "There are times I just like to be alone."

"You feel bad about Colin's drowning, don't you?" he asked.

"Yes," I said. "I didn't really know Colin Ledger, but from what I've seen of him, I thought he was a nice man."

"Yes, I suppose so," said Larry. "Did you hear that he's going to be shipped back to Alice Springs to be buried? Seems he has some relatives who want it."

"That's interesting," I said. "I would have thought he would have liked to have been buried near the rock."

"Maybe he did want that," Larry said, "but you know relatives. And anyway, what difference can it make to him now?"

I did not comment on that. Larry changed the subject.

"Listen," he said, "what I really came here for was to ask you whether you'd like to go out in the Land Rover tomorrow. It would be fun just to spend a day or more riding around. How about it?"

"Well..." I said.

"Oh, come on, Melissa," he coaxed. "Don't worry. It's perfectly safe. The Land Rover is in good condition. I'm a good auto mechanic too and I have a good supply of food and water. And I even have a compass in case we get lost."

But I was already shaking my head. "No, thank you, Larry," I said. "I appreciate your asking me, but I'm not the Land Rover type. I'm a painter! Or I hope to be."

"It would be good for you to see a little of the country," Larry said. "Don't you want to see the Great Outback of Australia?"

"Yes," I said. "Eventually, but not right now."

"Well," said Larry, "that's too bad because I think we could have a good time together."

"I'm sorry," I said, "but I'd probably be a lousy companion anyway."

"Well, I'm disappointed. I guess I'll just have to go and drown my sorrow by doing something crazy."

He left then. I closed and locked my door and went to bed. I was miserable. I lay there for a long time, half asleep. I could picture us driving through the wilderness, Larry's blond hair falling casually over his eyes—his bronzed skin alive.

I woke suddenly in the middle of the night. I could not recall what I had been dreaming or what my subconscious was working on, but my face was wet with tears and my throat choked with anguish.

I washed my face and tried to relax. When I awoke again, daylight was streaming through the cracks around the curtain and the door. I had missed the sunrise at the rock.

I got dressed and wandered over to the dining room. Doreen waved me over to her table. There she sat with Sylvia and Georgia, the three of them giggling conspiratorily.

"We saw the sunrise this morning!" Sylvia said.

"It was just gorgeous," raved Georgia.

"But we saw something else too," Doreen said. "We saw the girl Larry is going out in his Rover with. She just arrived last night."

"Wow, you should see her!"

Doreen leaned toward me. "Her name is Lynnette Werner," she said. "She's an American from San Francisco. She is something else. You should see her!"

"Hey, there she is!" Sylvia said, pointing at the window.

The three girls all moved their heads for a better look. I looked too.

They were right. Whoever Lynnette Werner was, she was something to see. She was wearing short shorts that showed as much as possible of her perfect legs, and a brief halter. Her long hair swished from side to side as she walked confidently.

I sipped my coffee, feeling miserable. No wonder Larry was going off with her. But he had asked me first! I could have gone.

"Looks like you have some real competition, Melissa," Georgia said.

"No competition," I said. "I'm not in any race."

But I didn't feel like eating and I left shortly afterwards.

I collected my painting materials and started off for the rock. I was determined to capture its likeness. But all I seemed to do was fool around with my palette and my brushes. What was the matter with me?

Yesterday I had had better luck when I went up closer to the rock. Maybe that would work today.

I wandered up close to the rock and looked around. I found another very small cave with nothing at all in it except some flashbulbs that some careless tourist had thrown away. I was annoyed. The rock to me was sacred. It seemed a shame to disfigure it with twentieth-century refuse.

I picked up the flashbulbs and put them in my pocket, just as a voice from behind me spoke. I jumped.

It was Frank. "I'm sorry that I frightened you."

"It's all right," I said. "It's so quiet and alone here. I just didn't expect to see anyone."

"I'm glad to see you." He looked at me seriously. "If you don't mind my asking, just what did you now find, some ancient prehistoric treasures?"

"No prehistoric treasures, I'm afraid," I said, showing him the flashbulbs. "Just some present trash."

"It's too bad people throw stuff away like that," he said.

"Are you exploring or painting this morning?" he asked, changing the subject.

"Well," I said, "I tried to paint, but I just can't seem to do much."

Frank laughed. "I heard there is such a thing as writer's block," he said, "but this is the first time I've heard of a painter's block. How do you propose getting past it?"

"Yesterday I looked at the rock a while, walking around it, and that helped, so I thought I'd try that again today."

"Do you mind if I go with you?" he asked.

"Of course not," I said.

He took my hand as we started along the side of the rock, straight into an angry group.

CHAPTER VII

As we rounded a corner of the rock we heard four people in a vicious argument. But it was very uneven, three against one.

All of the vivaciousness that Doreen, Sylvia, and Georgia brought to their laughter, they now brought to their fighting.

"It's hers," Georgia shouted. "Give it back!"

"It's mine," Sylvia wailed. "I found it!"

"Give it back, give it back, give it back," Doreen screamed over and over again.

Their opponent was Ralph Thompson, whom I had met yesterday. He stood there, trying hard to look innocent as he was confronted by the three girls.

Georgia saw us and ran over to us. "Melissa," she said. "Frank. Please help us. That man has stolen a rock that belongs to Sylvia."

"It's mine!" shouted Sylvia.

"Give it back!" Doreen shouted.

"Quiet, everybody," Frank said. "Now, one at a

time. Let's find out what's going on here. Sylvia, suppose you tell me your story."

Sylvia stopped wailing, took a deep breath, and tried to talk in a normal voice. "Well," she said, "we were walking along here looking at things when I found a strange rock. I was showing it to Georgia and Doreen, when this man came along. He walked by us, knocked the stone from my hand onto the ground, and then stole it!"

"No—" Ralph started.

"Yes, you did!" shouted Doreen.

"You took it!" Georgia yelled.

"Please be quiet, girls," Frank said. "Let Mr. Thompson tell his side of the story."

"All right," Ralph said, when the girls were quiet. "I did walk by when the girls were huddled together looking at something. And I did accidentally brush by Sylvia. I was too involved in my own thoughts and explorations, I guess. But I did not steal that stone. What would I want with a silly stone, when there are millions here all around?"

"Make him empty his pockets," said Doreen.

"I will not empty my pockets," Ralph Thompson said, "and I will not stay for more abuse."

He walked off. The girls continued to shriek.

"Aren't you making a big fuss over nothing?" Frank asked. "After all, he's right. There are a million stones around here."

"That was a special stone," Sylvia said. "As soon as I found it I knew it was special." I remembered another stone and got interested.

"Tell me about that stone," I said. "I found an interesting stone here at the rock the other day."

As Sylvia described it, I knew it was like the one I had found: dull gray, unusual.

"That's very strange," I said, "because I seem to have lost mine too."

"Why don't you look around more?" Frank said. "It may still be here somewhere. When you dropped it, it may have rolled into a crack."

"So you don't believe Ralph Thompson stole it," I said to Frank as we moved on.

"No, I don't," Frank said. "Why would he bother stealing a worthless stone?"

"Do you know this Thompson?" I asked.

"Well, a little."

Frank was quiet, preoccupied.

"I guess you'd rather not talk about him," I said.

"No, Melissa, I think I'll tell you about Thompson. I may need your help."

We found some large flat rocks and sat down. Frank looked at me quietly before he started talking. When he did so, he spoke slowly and seriously.

"I am an anthropologist," he said, "as you know. I study people like the aborigines. But I also like to study present-day people like you and me. I had a friend named Paul Morrison, who was also an anthropologist. His whole interest had shifted to present-day people. He had the idea of studying what kind of people come to see Ayers Rock. It's a tourist attraction, all right, but it has no beaches, no nightclubs, no great celebrities. All it is is a rock in a rather inaccessible place.

"So my friend Paul came here last year. He wrote me only one letter in which he told me that he had gotten into some very interesting situations. I came here to see what he meant. We talked a little, but he told me almost nothing.

"The second day after my arrival, he fell off the mountain."

"How terrible!" I said.

"Yes," said Frank, "it was. But it was the type of accident that happens here every so often. I just wish he could have told me more before he died. Then I could have understood some of the strange things that have happened since."

"Like what?"

"Well," said Frank, "immediately after Paul's death, four different men came here to see what happened to him. They all seemed to be looking for something, but I was never sure what. Ralph Thompson was one of them."

"Has he been here all this time?"

"No, no," said Frank. "He was here only a few days after Paul's death. I stayed a while myself and then I left. But he arrived back here the same day I did. It's uncanny. And he still seems to be looking for something."

"Rocks," I said. "Are there any valuable rocks or stones around here?"

"No," said Frank. "Some are unusual and pretty, but no valuable ones."

"Well," I said, "you said that perhaps I could help you. In what possible way? I'm new here myself. I know so little about this place."

"Yes," said Frank, "but you have an artist's eye. If you see that Thompson is doing anything unusual, you could let me know."

I shook my head. "I'm no spy," I said. "I'd hate to play one."

"All right," Frank said gently. "Forget it."

But it was the kind of thing I would not forget and he knew it. The closeness that had developed between us was broken. Frank became quiet and moody.

I excused myself. "Well," I said, "before the morning is over I have to do a little painting. For me, a day without painting is a day lost. Or something like that."

"OK," said Frank. "I'll see you later."

He kissed me lightly on the forehead and held my hand for a brief moment. And then he was gone.

I went back to my easel. Now I was able to paint. I worked on the rock and to my amazement and delight, it started to take on some personality. How could that rock be so alive, I wondered, when all it does is just stand there, century after century?

I mixed my paints over and over on the palette. What color was the rock? At times it was gray, but now it was more of a mauve. And then I remembered how it looked at sunrise and sunset.

After a while two elderly women came over to inspect my painting and offer advice. I had to figure out a way to get away from them.

"I'm just about to stop for lunch," I said. "Is there a bus going back to the hotel?"

"Yes," said one of the women. "And if we hurry, we can make it."

The bus joggled us back to the hotel. Once there, I was met by the three girls.

"Did you ever find your stone?" I asked Sylvia.

"What?" she asked, confused.

"Your stone, the one you dropped?"

Doreen turned to Sylvia. "You know that stone that Thompson guy stole?"

"Oh, that!" Sylvia said. "No, I didn't, but it doesn't matter."

"I thought you cared about that stone."

"No," Sylvia said, "the stone didn't matter. I just didn't like having a creep like Thompson steal it."

I ate hurriedly, somehow feeling too old for these girls. What was it about me that made me seem so much older? Maybe it was the spirit of comradeship they had among themselves. I had nothing, no one.

I left the dining room feeling very sorry for myself. Well, I would get back to my painting as soon as possible. After all, that was the one thing I did have.

But as I left the dining room I saw Catherine sitting all alone in her wheelchair. I approached her softly, but she heard me.

"Is that you, Melissa?"

"Yes."

"You sound very unhappy."

"Well," I said, "unhappy's not the word. I guess I'm just feeling lonely."

"You don't have to be lonely, you know," Catherine said. "There are many people here offering you their friendship."

"Yes," I said. "I guess I'm not sure I want it."

"So," said Catherine. "Of course, that is your choice. Maybe you'd rather be lonely."

I smiled then and laughed softly. "I guess there are times when I do prefer loneliness, unfortunately."

Catherine reached out her thin hand and held mine. "Do be careful, Melissa, that you don't let your loneliness deceive you into accepting any friendship that is not real."

But now Catherine seemed to be more or less talking to herself. "Colin made the mistake of being too honest, too trusting. He knew too much, too many secrets. Someone killed him because of all he knew."

"Someone killed Colin!" I exclaimed.

"Oh, yes," said Catherine. "Of course, no one will ever be able to prove it. But I knew Colin. I knew what kind of man he was. I knew he could never drown by accident. That man would have had to be killed."

Tears were running down her cheeks. I leaned over and touched her gently on the shoulder.

"I'm sorry," I said, not knowing what to say.

"And his relatives are not even going to allow him to be buried here," she moaned. "Colin's whole life was here at the rock. When they take his body away tomorrow, they will take away a part of me too."

She turned her head to me and spoke sternly. "Melissa, now go. Run along, get back to your paints. But be careful. Make a choice between loneliness and love, but don't choose the wrong love!"

"I'll be careful," I said, "but people have only offered me friendship, not love."

"They will," said Catherine firmly. "They will."

CHAPTER VIII

I took my paints and went back to the rock, where I set up my easel and tried to get a good view. The rock was fantastic. It filled the landscape and reminded me of the foundation of the world. Civilizations would come and go but this rock would exist forever.

Now I was inspired. I filled in the rock, letting it possess the canvas. I worked at it all afternoon and, when I was finished, I was satisfied.

The evening sky was starting to grow red as I realized that I wanted to see the sunset tonight.

I found the same quiet place where Frank and I had watched the sunset last night. But Frank was nowhere in sight, and I had the place all to myself.

And I was disappointed. The sun flitted among the clouds for a while, but eventually it just gave up. It set without kissing the rock good night.

I could not stop looking at the rock, even though it was now not much more than a huge black hulk in the night. Finally I left to go back to the hotel.

In the darkness I hurried back as fast as I could.

Once I thought I heard footsteps behind me. I stopped and listened, but I could see or hear nothing. And yet later I thought I heard them again.

I felt a deep sense of relief as I saw the lights of the hotel ahead. Soon I would be in its sheltering walls. But the hotel lights threw huge, frightening shadows on every building and object in their path. I was completely out of breath by the time I reached the hotel.

Frank stood near the door. He looked at me quizzically. "What's the matter, Melissa? You look as if you've seen a ghost."

"Well," I said, smiling in my relief, "I haven't seen any ghosts, but I found out that it can be mighty scary out there in the dark."

"You really shouldn't go out there alone," Frank said. "It's just not safe."

"I guess my imagination was working overtime," I said. "I would think that Ayers Rock must have one of the lowest crime rates in the world."

"I suppose it does," Frank said, "but it does seem to have an extraordinary number of accidents."

"Yes, I guess I should play it safe," I said, and then suddenly and inexplicably felt depressed.

"Let's eat," Frank said. "But I guess first you want to put your paints away."

He walked me to my room, waited outside while I refreshed myself, and then walked me to supper. All during the meal we talked, and he was thoughtful and attentive.

"Well," he said, as we finished eating, "would you like to walk around outside a while? It's turning into a nice evening after all."

And it was. The moon was out now and the stars

twinkled. Frank took my arm in his. "Melissa," he said, "you are really a very attractive girl."

"Well, thank you," I said.

"No, I mean it," he said. "Let's stop here and rest a bit."

We were then out by a pile of rocks near the rock. It looked manmade, with all kinds of rocks thrown on top of one another, but according to the information in the guidebook, it had been like that as long as anyone could remember.

I sat down on one of the flat rocks. Frank sat next to me with his arm around me. Then he slowly leaned over and gave me a tender kiss. It was beautiful. But somehow I wasn't quite in the mood. I moved over a little.

"I'm sorry if I offended you," he said.

"No," I said, "you didn't offend me. Let's explore a little."

"All right," said Frank. "Let's climb up this pile of rocks."

I looked at it. "Is it safe?"

"Of course it is," he said. "There was never a tourist who fell off this pile and got hurt!"

"Well, just remember that I'm not a tourist," I said.

But climbing the pile was not as easy as I thought it would be. The rocks proved to be slippery and I kept on losing my foothold.

"I guess I'm just not a climber," I said.

Frank said, "If you'd rather not climb, it's quite all right."

For just a minute I almost decided not to climb up, but then something came into my mind: the image of Larry with Lynnette. I could see the two of them climbing this pile, laughing all the way up.

I climbed. Frank stayed near me the whole time. In a little while we were at the top, the two of us looking down at the ground and then across the way at Ayers Rock.

"Why, this is nice," I said. "The first mountain I've ever climbed."

"It won't be the last, I hope," said Frank.

We stood hand in hand at the top of the pile. Frank kissed me again and this time I did not resist. But there was no magic in it, and I felt profoundly disappointed in myself. After all, Frank was so good and kind to me. Why did I feel nothing for him?

After a while I decided that it was time to leave.

Frank helped me down. Then we walked hand in hand back to the hotel. His hand was warm and gentle, but I found my thoughts wandering.

"Tomorrow I guess I'll try to capture Ayers Rock at night," I said. "I'll work out the background by day and then tomorrow night I'll try to fill in the rock as I see it by the light of the moon."

I was suddenly aware that I was so engrossed in my plans that I hadn't heard Frank speak.

I felt miserable, and I knew that I had made him miserable too.

He took me to my room and said good night. But he did no more than plant a light kiss on my forehead.

I slept fitfully that night, not able to quite get over the empty, disappointed feeling that I had had all day.

I got up before dawn because I wanted to see the sunrise again. I walked out to the rock alone. In the early morning I was not afraid. It was still quite dark but there were a million stars that seemed very close to the earth. With so little artificial light and no industry, there was nothing to hinder their light.

And then I was at the rock. The tourist bus pulled up about the same time I did. Everyone positioned himself to see the rock, and this morning the show was wonderful. For a very short time the sun bathed the rock in glowing golds and warm yellows. And then the sun rose and the spell was broken.

I walked slowly back to the hotel. I rather liked being alone, savoring the glory of the vision I had just seen.

Just as I arrived at the hotel, a Land Rover arrived. Before I even saw the occupants I knew who they were, and my spirits took a tumble.

Larry and Lynnette had returned.

I went into the dining room hoping that they had not seen me. I couldn't bear to meet Larry just now.

Frank saw me as I entered and called me over. "Come and eat with me," he said.

"All right," I said, listlessly.

"How was the sun this morning?" he asked, trying to make pleasant conversation. "I didn't get up in time to see it."

"It was glorious," I said, watching the door. "Beautiful. The best I've seen yet."

And then we both fell silent and ate.

Larry and Lynnette did not come into the dining room. I should have known they wouldn't.

"Are you feeling all right?" Frank asked after a while.

"Yes," I said.

"You look pale or something," he said.

"I'm all right," I said. "But now I think I'd better go. I want to get a good start on my painting today."

"Yes, your painting," Frank said. "Well, have a good day."

I collected my painting materials and set out. I

walked fast, angry and upset. I almost knocked Larry down.

"Melissa," he said, "where are you going in such a hurry?"

"Out to paint," I gasped.

"Oh, yes, to paint," he repeated. "Melissa, you should have gone with me yesterday, I had a great time."

"I'm sure you did," I said, "but apparently you didn't need me."

Larry laughed softly and his blue eyes sparkled. "I do believe you're jealous," he said. "Well, how about that?"

"I am not," I said. "I really don't have time to waste here."

I started to leave, then stopped and turned briefly. "Really, Larry," I said. "I'm glad that you had a nice trip yesterday."

He smiled at me and said, "Thanks, Melissa."

Just then Lynnette came around the corner. "Larry," she shouted. "Come, let's get something to eat before they close the dining room."

And they were gone, walking arm in arm.

I took my paints and hurried on. I had planned on painting the moonlit rock, but now I couldn't do it. The soft colors just didn't fit my mood.

So I tried painting the rock as it had been in the morning, but my golds and yellows came out much stronger than I had expected. After a while I put my paints down and stopped.

"Melissa," said a voice behind me, "let's go and climb the rock."

It was Larry, his eyes sparkling again.

I looked him straight in the eye. "All right," I said. "Let's climb it!"

CHAPTER IX

We climbed the rock. Larry went on ahead, and I followed, all the time struggling, slipping, and scared. The first part of the climb was easy. For a while I could take it step by step from one rock to another, each just a footstep apart. Then the climb got steeper and I began having doubts. Just at that point the chain started. Someone, sometime, had fastened a chain along the side of the rock so that climbers like me would have something to hold on to. Larry waited for me at the beginning of the chain.

"How are you doing, Melissa?" he asked.

"Fine," I said, huffing and puffing. "I'm not an experienced climber, you know."

"You're doing fine," he said, "but here is where I think I should let you go ahead. I'll follow you."

"Thanks," I said, "I'll feel safer that way."

I held on to the chain and moved upward. If this steep and slippery side was the tourist side, what were the other sides like?

Finally the chain came to an end and we were on our

53

own. I scrambled up, with Larry close behind me. Then, suddenly, we were at the top.

The top was nearly flat, and I tried to stand up straight. The wind caught me and pushed hard.

"Be careful," said Larry. "That wind is strong. You've heard about people being blown off the top here."

"Yes," I said, "I have. But don't you think that was a special wind, a tornado or something?"

"No," said Larry, "just an ordinary wind. But they must have been near the edge or lost their footing. The wind feels strong, but it's not going to pick you up and carry you off like in the Wizard of Oz."

"I hope not."

"Let's explore a bit," he said, taking my hand. The view was fantastic. We could see for miles.

Larry told me, "They say that in clear weather you can see for hundreds of miles. But of course, it doesn't seem like that, since the land around here is so flat and uniform. Everywhere you look you see the same low bushes, rough, uneven ground, and small, scraggly trees."

"Right," I said, "except over there."

I pointed in the direction of some mountains.

"Those are the Olgas," Larry said. "I guess you haven't seen them close up yet."

"No," I said, "I haven't. I wanted to get acquainted with Ayers Rock first before I let myself get involved with other mountains."

Larry looked at me seriously. "You're pretty careful about getting yourself involved in anything, aren't you?"

I looked at him but did not answer. He didn't expect one.

After a while I began to feel frightened. "I'd like to go down," I said. "I have a feeling that going down is going to be even harder than going up."

"Well, you're right about that," he said. "But I'm not ready to go down yet. First, there's this."

He held me close and kissed me, a kiss warm and tender, yet so powerful that it took my breath away.

"Now, fair lady," he said, "let's go. I'll lead the way and you follow. That way I'll be below you and ready to catch you if you fall. But you won't, of course. Just remember that you have to descend backwards."

We went down slowly. I felt very insecure all the way, but below me was Larry. It seemed he never took his eyes off me. All the time his blue eyes seemed to be watching. And caring, I hoped.

I felt thrilled with his kiss. But visions of him laughing and going with Lynnette filled my mind. He must have noticed my preoccupation because he spoke to me, puzzled.

"Are you all right?" he asked. "You're not frightened, are you?"

"No, I'm not frightened," I said. I didn't know how to tell him how angry I was.

At last we were at the bottom. Larry took my hand. "Well," he said, "believe it or not, you've missed your lunch at the dining room. Come, let me take you somewhere to lunch."

I laughed at that. "Like where?" I asked, knowing very well that there was nowhere to go.

"Like in my Land Rover," Larry said. "I carry a full supply of interesting food there at all times."

But the Land Rover made me think of Lynnette, and I could not go there. What if she had left some personal things behind?

"Thank you," I said, "but I'm not really very hungry. I appreciate climbing with you, but now I think I'd better get back to my painting."

"Your painting," he said. He looked at it and said, "I must say, it's very good."

"You don't have to say that," I said. I was tired of unknowledgeable people who came up to compliment me when they knew nothing about painting.

"I never say things I don't mean," Larry said, and then he was gone.

Whatever else could be said about Larry, he did something to me. He made me want to do and try things. I began to glimpse some of the feeling of life he had. And I envied him for that. I envied Lynnette for her gift of life.

I worked at my painting with renewed feelings. I put on the paints with abandon, let them absorb me, let them have a life of their own, until the painting was complete and the rock shone out with full life. The rock was alive, no doubt about that.

Suddenly I realized that it was getting dark. And I did not want to miss the sunset. But I felt cold and frightened. Something was not right. I was all alone, but suddenly I knew that someone was watching me.

I turned around quickly. A man tried to hide as I turned, but he quickly realized that I had seen him and stepped out.

"Why . . . ?" I said, recognizing Ralph Thompson.

"I didn't mean to frighten you," he said.

"But you did," I said.

"I'm sorry." He looked contrite. "Let's make up. Can I walk you over to the site to see the sunset?"

I felt a distinct sense of warning, a foreboding. But I

did not know any way of getting out of it. After all, should I miss the sunset for some irrational feeling?

"All right," I said. "And we'd better hurry. It will be setting soon."

He took my arm as we walked, and slowly started to question me.

"You went climbing with Larry O'Brien this morning?" he asked.

"Why, yes," I said.

"Did you have a good time?"

"Of course."

"Seems like you and Larry are getting to be good friends."

I stopped. "Larry and I went climbing on the rock. Period."

"Ah," said Ralph, "you are angry. But I think Larry means more to you than that."

"If you want to see someone Larry is fond of, why don't you see Lynnette?"

Ralph laughed a low, slow laugh, "Aha!" he said. "Now I know you care. But I want to tell you something. Be careful. Be wary of Larry. He will hurt you."

"What do you mean?" I asked angrily.

"I can't tell you now," he said, "but Larry is not to be trusted. You should keep away from him."

"Well, if you aren't going to tell me why, you can just go on yourself," I said. "Larry means nothing to me. But if he did it still wouldn't be any of your business."

I walked off, but inside I was trembling. My concern for Larry was a little too obvious.

Later I watched the sunset, my angry mood not dissipating until the fullness of the gold and yellow was upon the rock. Then I started to feel warmer and less angry. Two thoughts surfaced.The first was that I cared about Larry and that perhaps others thought he cared about me. Would that that were true!

The second was the chilling thought that Ralph Thompson might know something about Larry that I should know. I knew almost nothing about Larry, except that he was full of life and had a gift of laughter and fun that I wished I had. With him I could pick up the sparks of that kind of life.

I was not thinking pleasant thoughts as the bus driver shouted at me. "Miss Carrington, would you like a ride back to the hotel?"

"Yes, thank you," I called. I got on the bus and took a quick look around. Ralph Thompson was not there. He must have walked back by himself.

But as we passed the rock on our way home, I saw a shadowy figure. Ralph? What was he looking for?

When we got back to the hotel I went to my room to put my equipment away. My mind was in a turmoil. There was so much I wanted, so much, but I didn't really know what it was. All I knew right now was that I was very hungry. No wonder, I had skipped lunch. But before I went to the dining room, I looked at the two paintings I had done of Ayers Rock so far. Of the two the second was far better, much more full of life. The first seemed lifeless, and yet I had been pleased with it at the time. Well, tomorrow I would start on my next painting.

On the way to the dining room, I saw old Catherine, again talking to tourists.

"You will find something special here at the rock," she was telling a young woman.

"Something special, or some*one* special?" the young woman squealed. And then I saw who it was. Lynnette.

I approached Catherine as Lynnette rushed off. "Hello, Catherine," I said.

"It is Melissa, the young American painter," she said. "I am glad to see you again."

"And I you. I hope that you're feeling somewhat better. I wanted to tell you that I sympathize with your loss of Colin."

She was silent for a while. "No one will ever know what Colin meant to me," she said finally. "But you, Melissa, I have strange feelings about. Be careful. You are still in danger. Somehow I feel your danger is connected to Colin. Though how, I don't know. I just see you in the same aura of death that I see Colin in."

"But I have never felt more alive than I did today," I said. "I even climbed the rock."

"Oh, Melissa," she said, "please be careful. Heed my words. There is some kind of danger threatening you."

I murmured my thanks and left. But I knew I could not let her vague prophecy order my life.

As I entered the dining room the first thing I saw was Larry and Lynnette together at a table. There were others at the table too, but Larry was the center of attention. He saw me and beckoned.

"Come over and join us, Melissa," he said. "There's room here."

I shook my head. I couldn't bear to eat with him and Lynnette. I could not bear to be ignored by both of them. Not after this afternoon.

The three giggly girls waved at me but there was no room at their table. The only vacant space I saw was at a table with three elderly women.

Well, I said to myself, I guess that's it. The women were gushing over the rock. Finally one of them said, "We just came from Coober Pedy today."

"Coober Pedy?" I said. "Is that where they have the opal mines?"

"It is indeed. We even visited the mines and at the shop I bought an uncut opal."

She fumbled in her purse. "Would you like to see it?" she asked.

I nodded.

"It's uncut," she went on, "but still it cost too much. But I thought it would be a nice gift for my son. He can get it cut and give it to his wife."

She opened a small box from her purse and pulled out the uncut opal. I recognized it. It was just like the strange stone I had found. The stone that had disappeared from my room.

CHAPTER X

The next few days went by uneventfully. Every day I was busy painting, painting, painting. Each morning I rose before dawn to see the rock, and each day it was different. But always it lived. Each evening I went to see the sunset. Sometimes it was a brilliant gold; at other times it was more somber, almost a deep violet. And one evening it was a brilliant red, so brilliant that I despaired of ever capturing it on my canvas.

My painting was not going well. The rock was so hard to capture. But I refused to let it conquer me. I worked at it every day, and that was about all I did.

I did not see Larry. I did not see Frank. I did not even see Ralph Thompson. The three giggly girls had left, but they solemnly promised one and all that they would return. I knew they would be back—they were hoping to find something or someone here.

I knew exactly how they felt, I felt the same deep yearning for someone.

The evenings were almost unbearable. I spent them in my room, planning the next day's painting and going to bed early. Since Colin's death, a young man had taken over showing slides for the tourists. But I did not want to attend. I was still deeply disturbed by Colin's death. In my heart I believed, like Catherine, that his death was no natural one.

Besides my loneliness, a deep sense of foreboding bothered me. I knew that a new disaster was on the wing, one that I would have a definite part of.

Catherine had foretold it and in my heart of hearts I believed her. At times I felt I should leave all this behind. But I could not. I wanted to stay. I told myself that I wanted to stay because I wanted to paint, really, but I wanted to stay because Larry was here. If he left permanently, maybe I would leave too.

I stayed in my room in the evening because I had nothing to do elsewhere. Secretly I hoped that Larry would come and knock at my door. But he did not. And I couldn't bear to go out and see if I could "accidentally" run into him. I was afraid that I would find him in the arms of Lynnette. Or somebody else. He likes all girls, I thought. And I felt chagrined that I was just another of the girls he had charmed. I wanted to be somebody special to him.

And I was deeply disturbed by the fact that that opal had been taken from my room. But by whom? Who even knew I had it?

Since I thought so much of Larry I remembered every incident with him. I remembered with dismay the conversation he had with Ralph Thompson—he promised Ralph something, but wanted some "goodies" for himself too. What kind of goodies? Opals?

I knew nothing about Larry. He wouldn't be the first handsome man to turn out to be a thief.

My painting showed the effects of all this conflict. How could I capture the long-standing serenity of the rock when I was in so much turmoil?

But on the third day I found out how. I was out trying to paint when suddenly the sky grew very dark. Rain was coming. There was no shelter. I hurried over to the rock, lugging my easel, my paints, and the wet canvas.

I sat down in one of the shallow caves and watched the rain rush down the sides of the rock. I was relatively safe and secure in the cave. When the rain pelted the edges and the spray hit me, I moved further into the cave.

There were dim lines on the cave's back wall. Why, these are paintings, I realized. I knew from the guidebooks and from Dennis that these were probably nothing other than sketches aborigines had made under circumstances very much like my own. Hiding from a storm, they drew pictures to while away the time. Not a bad idea at all.

I set up my easel near the entrance and started to paint. What I wanted to do now was to draw the rock as it looked when it was being pelted by rain under the dark clouds.

The light was not good, but I painted on and on. I felt a deep sense of peace pervading me. Soon I had almost finished. I looked at the painting. No, it was not really good, but it was the best I had done recently. Its silver and gray lines showed something of how I felt and how the rock looked right now.

There was more light. I moved back into the darkness of the cave to have a second look at the drawings. They were hard to make out. There were lines, straight and crooked, circles and ovals. Nothing definite, nothing finished, more like doodles on a telephone pad than any kind of symbolic drawings.

But near the bottom of the wall was something else.

It was very small, easily overlooked and appeared to be a kind of map, complete with an X to mark the spot. What spot? I wondered. And then I smiled to myself. This was probably drawn the day before yesterday by some tourist. I was surprised not to see a flourishing initial in a corner.

"What are you doing?" someone asked. I jumped.

It was Frank, just entering the cave. His face showed fear for just a moment. Then it relaxed into a smile.

"Why, Frank," I said, "it's good to see you."

"You too," he said. "What are you doing in this damp cave?"

"Well," I said, "I came in here to get out of the rain."

"And you painted," he said. "May I look?" But he was already looking. He nodded approvingly.

"This is good work," he said. "I do believe that you've captured some of the gloom and sadness of a rainy day at Ayers Rock."

"I hope so," I said. "That was what I was trying to do."

"Aren't you afraid of the rainbow serpent?"

"What's that?" I asked.

"Well," said Frank, "I would think that this kind of day, with the rain just over and the sun coming out and a possibility of a rainbow existing, would be just the day for him to be around. There is, according to old legends, a rainbow serpent who lives down here, under the water at the base of the rock. He'll come out and devour you if you're not careful."

I laughed a little. "No," I said, "I haven't seen any serpents at all, rainbow or otherwise."

"Come and see the Olgas after the rain," he said, taking my hand and pulling me toward the front of the cave.

We looked in the direction of the Olgas. They were

beautiful, silver-gray and glistening in the evening sun.

"Would you like to go there to see them tomorrow?" Frank asked.

"Yes, I would," I said. "I've been painting steadily for three days now and haven't really had much luck. Maybe I would do just as well to take a day off and enjoy the Olgas. Some people like them even better than the rock, I hear."

"Yes," Frank said, "I like them too. But not as much as Ayers Rock. And I suspect you won't either."

"We shall see," I said.

Frank took my hand. "Let's go watch the sunset," he said. "Here, let me take your easel. I have my car out here. We can put them in it, and then go and see the rock."

"Oh," I said, "I didn't even know you had a car."

"Yes, I have," Frank said, "but normally I prefer to walk or use the bus. That rain put a damper on the idea of walking over here."

In a little while we reached Frank's car and drove to the site where we had seen the sunset previously.

"It might be beautiful tonight," Frank said. "The old-timers tell us that it's at its best after a rain."

"Old-timers like Colin?" I asked.

"Yes," said Frank, looking concerned.

I pursued it. "Old Catherine thinks that his death was no accident, that he was pushed or deliberately drowned."

Frank looked at me very seriously. "No," he said firmly, "his death was an accident. Catherine should be careful not to spread false rumors like that."

The sunset was marvelous, full of silver and gold in incredible combinations. At one minute it was solid silver, a minute later, pure gold.

"Breathtaking, isn't it?" asked Frank.

"Yes," I said simply.

Then Frank leaned over and kissed me gently, but somehow I felt nothing. No magic.

When we drove back to the hotel, we talked little.

"Well," said Frank, "still want to go to the Olgas tomorrow?"

"Yes," I said, "and I appreciate your taking me there."

"Good," Frank said. "Can I take you to dinner now?"

"That would be lovely," I said. "But first let's take care of all these paints and materials."

As I freshened up for dinner, I was feeling desperate. I must have some kind of perverse nature, I thought. I can't even get interested in a man who is so kind to me. I don't know what it is about him, but Frank simply didn't excite me.

And yet I was so lonely.

Dinner was a pleasant-enough affair. Frank was attentive to me, thoughtful and valiant at making an effort to talk to me about anything that I wished.

He was an interesting conversationalist and I tried my best to be the charming dinner companion he deserved. Well, I said to myself, in this case I will have to follow my head and not my heart. At least he is intellectually stimulating.

But I forgot my resolve a few seconds later, when Larry entered the dining room all alone. He looked in my direction, started to come over, and then noticed Frank leaning close to me.

Larry turned away. And my heart ached.

CHAPTER XI

Finally supper was over. I did not look again at Larry; I tried to be attentive to Frank. But all the time I regretted the fact that Frank's presence had kept Larry from coming over to me. I so much wanted to see him.

After supper Frank and I went for a walk. After the rain of the day, the air was clearer and the stars were bright. It was a beautiful evening. If I had been with Larry I would have counted myself the most fortunate person alive. As it was, I felt miserable. But Frank was kind and I tried to be nice to him.

"I'll pick you up right after breakfast," he said. "Are you planning to see the sunrise?"

"Maybe," I said. "It will depend on how I feel when I wake up."

But I knew that I would get up for the sunrise. I just wanted to be alone for it in the early morning.

I did not sleep well that night. My loneliness seemed even worse after the evening with Frank.

I got up early in the chilly morning, dressed warmly, and quietly made my way out to the rock. I loved being alone then, in the quiet, star-lit morning, the velvet darkness. There was a magic in the rock at sunrise. With a smile I remembered the guide telling us that sunset was always better than sunrise. How wrong he was! It was the sunrise that I preferred, because it seemed each morning to be like the dawn of creation.

I found my favorite vantage spot near the rock and waited. This morning the sunrise was the best I had ever seen. But it didn't start that way.

The sky was cloudy, and there was a bit of mist in the air. The sun seemed to have a hard time making it through the clouds. It cast a timid glow on the world, then disappeared again as if it wasn't sure that it really wanted to rise.

From the hill where a few tourists huddled I could hear muttered disappointment. Already a few people were closing their camera cases and heading back to the bus. Some people leave everything early, I mused. And what they missed! Just then, when we thought we had missed the sunrise, it shone through with full splendor on the rock. The rock smiled back at it, cooing for all the world like a beloved child. And then, above the rock, a rainbow was clearly visible.

It was beautiful beyond words. I stood in awe for quite a while, glad to be alone, glad to have a chance to see this wonder of nature, to savor its beauty. Then a jarring note broke into my consciousness. What was it that Frank had told me about rainbows? About rainbow snakes? I hadn't even asked him what rainbow snakes were, whether they were poisonous or not.

And then I started walking back to the hotel. The thought of poisonous snakes had ruined my image of the rainbows. I was lost in thought when I heard footsteps behind me. I turned quickly. Larry! My heart lit up the way the rock had done with the sun.

"Larry!" I exclaimed happily.

"Melissa!" he imitated. Then, "May I walk you back to the hotel?"

"Why, yes," I said. "I'd like that."

He took my hand. "You know, it's not very safe to walk alone like this in the dark."

"I'm not afraid," I said. "Somehow the morning is so beautiful I feel secure."

"Be careful," Larry said, half jokingly. "Beautiful things are not always safe."

We chatted pleasantly until we got to the hotel. "I hope you're having good luck painting," Larry said. "Maybe today you'll let me see your creation."

"Not today," I said. "I won't be doing any painting today."

"Oh?" said Larry. "What are you going to do, some exploring? Maybe I could go with you."

"No," I said sadly. "Today I'm going to visit the Olgas."

"Oh, I see," said Larry. "Well, then I guess I'll see you tomorrow." With that he left. I felt drained and miserable.

I ate breakfast with some new tourists. They were full of fanciful stories about the rock.

"Is is true," one asked, "that there are prehistoric drawings in the caves of ancient astronauts?"

"Well," I said, "I've seen the caves, but I didn't really see any ancient drawings. There are many drawings there, but most of them, I think, were done rather recently."

Something in my own words bothered me, and then

I remembered the drawing I had been looking at when Frank came in and asked what I was doing.

I pulled myself back to the conversation. My concern for Larry and my conflicting feelings about Frank were interfering with my rational processes. I was allowing myself to become too suspicious.

I finished eating and left. I was straightening up things in my room when there was a knock on the door.

"Is that you, Frank?" I called.

"No, it's Ralph Thompson. Could I talk to you for a few minutes, please?"

I was surprised. "Well," I said, "all right, I'll be with you in a minute."

"Can I come inside a minute?" he asked warily as I opened the door. It was as if he was afraid of being seen talking to me.

"Why, yes," I said, "but I'm expecting someone else soon."

"Who, Frank?"

"Yes," I said. "Well, what can I do for you?"

Ralph said, "I want to talk to you about an opal."

"Yes," I said guardedly. "What about an opal?"

"Well—" He seemed to hesitate. "Doreen, you remember her?"

"Yes," I said.

"She told me that you too had found an uncut opal."

"Was that what you took from the girls that day at the rock?" I blurted out.

"Yes," he said carefully, "but that is a long story. There's a lot more here than meets the eye. Please, can you tell me where you found that opal?"

"I hardly remember," I said. "Anyway, someone came in here and took it, so whatever it's worth, it's gone now."

"Those uncut opals are not worth much," Ralph said. "Even as cut stones, unless they're unusually large or unusually cut, their value is considerably less than that of a diamond or some other really precious stone."

"So what is all this about?"

"I need to know where you found that opal," he said, "because then I can find the answer to another problem I'm working on."

"Well, you can go on working out your problems without bothering Melissa!" Frank broke in angrily from the doorway.

Ralph looked perturbed. "Melissa," he said, "I'm not trying to bother you." He rose to go. "But if you happen to remember where you found that opal, please let me know. I'll be here at the rock for a while." Then he left and Frank turned to me.

"What was all that about an opal?"

"Oh," I said, trying to sound nonchalant, "I can't remember where I found an uncut opal that I apparently lost later, and that Ralph tells me has no value anyway. Come on, let's go. I'm anxious to see the Olgas."

We set off. I knew Frank wanted to know more, but I had no intention of telling him. He was a good sport, however, and soon began explaining things to me as we rode in his car.

"Ayers Rock is 2,870 feet above sea level," he said. "It's situated on land that is already high above sea level. But I like to think that it has a deep foundation. It is as deep as it is high. A rock with a foundation like that will last forever. No wonder the aborigines had tales about a rainbow serpent living down below. I guess they figured that there was plenty of space down there for some huge beast."

"But rainbows are beautiful," I said. "There was a beautiful rainbow above the rock this morning."

"Ah," said Frank, "you saw the sunrise."

"I did indeed," I said. "It was great. Worth getting up early for and walking over there in the darkness."

"You'd better be careful," Frank said. "That could be dangerous. Maybe you'd better take the bus from now on."

"Hmm," I said, not at all anxious to commit myself. Dangerous as it might be, I liked the early morning quiet and solitude.

But Frank was going on in his statistics. "The Olgas are quite a bit higher than the rock. The largest of the group is, of course, called Mt. Olga, and it's 3,419 feet above sea level. Quite high, you see."

"Yes," I said. "I didn't know that."

The Olgas were beautiful. They, along with the rock, were the only high spots on the vast and rough spinifex plain.

"The aborigines believed that all the world was completely flat," Frank said. "They believed that the earth always existed and was bald like an old man."

"So where did the rock and the Olgas come from?"

"Those," Frank said, "came later. They believed that those things, any kind of rocks or hills, or high elevations, or rivers or anything, were left behind by great men in the past. Some felt that the great men themselves made the high rocks; others felt that they were a kind of memorial to greatness.

"It's too bad," Frank went on, "that all these rocks and hills have European names. I personally think Uluru is a much nicer name than Ayers Rock, don't you?"

"Yes," I said. "Uluru is so much more gentle. How

about the Olgas? What were they originally?"

"Katajuta," said Frank, "meaning many heads. And a pretty good name at that, don't you think?"

I thought so, for the Olgas were less a single rock than a whole collection of mountains. In the morning sun they were ocher-colored and beautiful against a blue sky.

We got out of the car and looked around. The first thing we noticed was the strong wind pulling us.

"That's a powerful wind," I said. "I can imagine what it would be like on the tops of these mountains. It would be enough to blow you down."

"Yes, it would," Frank replied. "Maybe that's the reason why there are some peaks in this group that have never been climbed."

Frank took my arm then and we advanced toward the Olgas. Above us the mountains towered, Mt. Olga in the middle and her two leading councillors on either side. All three seemed to be plotting some disaster. As we walked toward them, I felt a chill and a premonition.

CHAPTER XII

The closer we got, the higher the Olgas looked, the more inaccessible. But they drew us like a magnet.

"Does this set of mountains have all the legends connected with it that Ayers Rock does?" I asked.

"Not as far as we know," said Frank. "Unfortunately, so much has been lost. The first people who met the aborigines thought of them as savages to be exterminated, and by the time people who cared about them had arrived, much of their heritage had been lost. There is so much about the aborigines that we don't know."

He sounded very sad and I warmed toward him. He seemed to be genuinely concerned about the aborigines.

"Let's do a little climbing," he said.

"All right," I said slowly, "but nothing very high. I'm a little frightened of this strong wind."

"OK," said Frank. "How about this little mountain here? See, the side is pretty slanty."

"Well," I said, "I'm willing to try."

And I did so, with Frank right behind me. At least his presence gave me some sense of security. We moved upward slowly. Although this might have been one of the easier mountains, the climb was still not easy. Soon I was huffing and puffing and moving one step after another with only the greatest of effort.

"Look," I said to Frank, "let's stop and rest a little. This ledge here is a good place."

"All right," he said, and we sat on the ledge and looked down. We had come a long way. Far below us was the road leading back to Ayers Rock. And, in the distance, was the rock itself.

"Do you know what some old-timers say that Ayers Rock looks like?" Frank asked.

"What?"

"A big slug."

"Well," I said, looking at it carefully, "I guess it does. But I don't like the description. After all, a slug isn't a very pleasant animal. I rather think it looks like a dog at rest."

Soon we got up and started to climb again, but it was hard to continue. The stop had made us lose our rhythm and we had to find it again.

We finally made it to the top, which was relatively flat.

"Here we are!" Frank exclaimed.

"Yes," I said, not daring to stand up straight. "This wind is terrible. I'm afraid it will blow me off."

"I don't think it will," Frank said, "but why don't you come over to the middle where it can't? Then you can stand up straight."

We were both soon at the center of the huge rock and looking out over all the world. Although Mt. Olga and her councillors still towered over us, we seemed to be on top of the world.

We stood there for a while, arm in arm, enjoying the view. The air was very clear and I remarked on it.

"Yes," said Frank, "but it's questionable whether or not it will remain that way. This area may be developed into a mining site. They don't know yet whether there are any mineral deposits here worth the trouble, but mineralogists are still looking. They may find something yet. And when and if they do, that will be the end of the clean air."

"How terrible!"

"Yes," said Frank, "and it's even worse than you think. If the mining companies don't do it, the tourist companies will. Do you know they're considering building more hotels here, even establishing some kind of viewing platforms to see the rock?"

I laughed bitterly. "Why not add an elevator to the rock and put a restaurant on top?"

"You laugh, but believe it or not, that idea has been seriously considered by some members of the government."

"Oh, no!"

We stayed a little longer, just looking. Down below I could see the miles of flat rugged land. The only thing marring the view was the road, a two-lane snake that wound its way across the country. Right now a car was approaching, the only vehicle besides a tourist bus on the road.

I looked closer. The car looked like a Land Rover. Could it be Larry's? Now it was closer. It stopped and a blond man got out. Larry! But he was not alone. A willowy young woman in shorts, her red hair tied casually with a scarf, was with him. Lynnette. I turned away.

Frank was watching me. "Are you ready to go down?" he asked.

"Yes," I said, "I think so. But is there another way down? Couldn't we go down on the other side?"

I just couldn't bear the thought of going down in Larry's presence.

"Well," said Frank, looking at me strangely, "let's take a look around. Let's see what the other sides look like."

We found that although the way we had come up was the best, we could probably get down on the opposite side. It was slightly steeper, but not too bad.

"The only thing you'll have to watch is that you don't slip," Frank said. He started down before me, to save me in case I slipped, he said laughingly. I followed, moving backward slowly and gingerly. The first part was not hard and I was starting to feel less uneasy about the climb when suddenly, my right foot slipped. I held on with both hands, while I tried to get my right foot back in place. Frank put his arms around me until I felt secure again.

"Relax," he said gently. "You're all right. You'll make it."

After that the climb got harder. I moved slower and slower. "Do you want to stop and rest a little?" Frank asked. "There's a ledge just a few feet down."

I hesitated a moment. "No, I'm afraid that if we stop I'll have a hard time getting going again."

"Well," said Frank, "I guess you're right." And we kept on the torturous climb.

But then something happened that I certainly did not expect. Frank slipped and skidded down several feet.

I stopped and looked down. He was clinging to the side of the mountain.

"Are you all right?" I called.

"Yes," he said, between gasps. "That slide just took the wind out of me."

Now it was my turn. "Relax," I said, "until you feel better."

"Be careful," he warned. "There's a bad spot in there."

I tried to go down, but without Frank's reassuring presence below me, I could not move. The more I realized that he had slipped, the more paralyzed I became.

Meanwhile Frank was moving on down. Then he turned and looked up. "Are you all right, Melissa?" he called. "Come on, it's not that far down."

"I'm afraid," I said. "I can't move."

"I'll wait for you," Frank said. "Come on."

"I can't move."

"Yes, you can." I could tell that he was trying hard to keep a note of panic out of his voice. "Shall I wait or what would you like?" he asked finally.

"You go on," I said. "I'll come when I can. But I can't move right now."

Frank hung there for a while, and then he slowly descended to the ground. I stayed where I was.

Once I tried to reach out my foot to find a lower resting place, but I quickly returned it to where it was. I could already picture myself sliding down the rest of the mountain.

"Frank," I whimpered. He was now at the bottom looking up.

"Come on, try it," he shouted up at me. "You can make it. Come on, please."

I said nothing. Just hung there.

"You can make it," he shouted. "You can make it. Just take it step by step."

I held there, fear growing every minute. I couldn't move, but I also couldn't hold on much longer. And then I heard a familiar voice below. Larry's voice echoed up to me. I turned my head slightly and saw him talking to Frank.

"Melissa!" Larry shouted. "Come on, try to get down. We'll help you."

He started up after me.

Suddenly I could move. Slowly I moved my foot down and found a place to put it. Then I lowered my other foot and the rest of my body. My hands no longer felt so numb.

Bit by bit I was able to descend. At the same time Larry was coming up until he was right below me.

"Take it easy," he said gently to me. "Take it easy. You can make it."

He backed his way down and I followed him. The climb was still painful, but I could make it. I climbed step by painful step, and finally we were on the ground.

Once there, I lowered myself to the ground and felt miserable. I turned to Larry. "Thank you, Larry, for helping me." There was so much I wanted to say, but that was all I could manage.

Frank looked at me sadly. "I'm sorry, Frank," I said. "I guess I'm a lousy mountain climber. I'm sorry that I spoiled your trip to the Olgas." And sorry for so many other things, I thought.

Frank tried to act casual. "That's all right," he said. "I'm not exactly a great mountain climber myself."

Larry said little, just looked at us.

But Lynnette broke in. "What I would like to know," she said, "is why you decided to come down this side of the mountain. It's pretty hard. The other side is much easier."

"Yes," said Frank, "but we went up that way."

"And you wanted some more variety?" asked Lynnette.

"Stupid, wasn't it?" I asked.

Lynnette turned to Larry. "Well," she said, "I guess these two are rescued. You've done your good deed for the day. Now, how about a few bad deeds with me? Let's go."

Larry gave her a half smile. "OK," he said, with a noticeable lack of enthusiasm. "Let's go."

"Wait," I said to Larry. "I want to thank you again. You saved my life. For the second time."

"That should mean something," he said softly. "Maybe someday we'll find out what it is."

They left then and Frank turned to me. "I guess I was something of a disappointment, wasn't I?" he said ruefully.

"Not really," I said. "Why should I assume that every man knows how to climb or do all kinds of things? My father was so good at repairing cars that I assumed all men knew all about cars. How wrong I was! And you know more about aborigines and people than many men." I meant my words to be warm and friendly and understanding, but Frank still looked hurt.

I took his hand. "It's all right," I said, and suddenly felt very much better.

CHAPTER XIII

We didn't stay long at the Olgas. Frank seemed aloof and preoccupied. I felt more tender toward him but was unable to break through his shell. So when he suggested we head back, I agreed.

After lunch, I said, "I think I'll paint this afternoon."

"All right," said Frank. "I'm anxious to get back to the caves and do some more exploring. I'll walk you over to the rock."

"That would be nice," I said. "I want to go to the south side. I haven't tried painting it yet and I have some ideas of what I could do with it."

Frank helped me carry my equipment as we walked over later. We were both rather quiet, and as soon as I got set up, Frank left.

"Thank you for a very nice morning," I called after him.

"You're welcome," he said. "I'm sorry that it turned out the way it did."

"It was all right," I said with a laugh. "What else do

people tell stories about, except accidents that almost happened?"

"Maybe that's one story that we'd do better forgetting," Frank said as he left.

The light was good today, and I was able to paint. I felt both sad and happy—why, I couldn't quite explain—and set about trying to get all of this into my picture.

Time passed, and I was so totally involved in my painting that I did not hear anyone approach. Then a man called out my name.

It was Ralph Thompson.

"Oh, hello," I said.

"Hello," he said, trying to act cheerful. "How's your painting today?"

"Just fine," I said, without stopping my work.

He was looking at it critically. "Yes," he said, "I do believe you're making progress."

I smiled a little to myself. After all, everyone always feels they have to tell an artist his work is good. He seemed to read my thoughts.

"I know what I'm talking about," he said. "I'm something of an artist myself. Or at least, a student of art. I never mastered some of the things that you seem to have mastered."

"Oh, really? I thought you were some kind of explorer or detective."

"Detective! Yes," he said seriously, "I guess I *have* come across that way. And I apologize. It's just that the company I work for sent me out here to find out some things."

"What company is that?" I asked. "I thought you told me you were a tourist."

"Well," he said, "my company asked me to combine a little business with pleasure."

"Wilson's," he said, without elaborating. "We operate out of Melbourne. And Melbourne is the center of art and culture in Australia, as you know."

"So I've heard," I said.

"But," Ralph went on, "while we're on the subject of detectives, do you remember now where you found that stone?"

"I think so," I said. "It was on the east side of the rock."

"Thank you very much," he said and started to leave.

I called him back. "Wait. Now I've told you something you wanted to know. How about you doing the same for me? Why did you tell me to keep away from Larry? What were you trying to warn me of?"

"Well," Ralph said, not meeting my eye, "I shouldn't have said that. I thought he was one of those playboys who try to get every pretty girl. But apparently you can take care of yourself."

And then he left. I had the distinct impression that he was withholding a lot more than he was telling me. But I went back to my painting, hoping that I would not be disturbed again.

But I was. This time it was Larry. He appeared as if from nowhere, climbing on the south side of the mountain. He moved into my line of vision and climbed upward, not seeming to notice anything or anybody. Then he turned, glancing over his shoulder. He saw me, and slowly, carefully, he made his way down.

"Well, hello, Melissa," he said. "What are you doing?"

"Well, as you can see," I said, "I'm painting. I've

nearly completed a new painting of this side of the rock."

"Wow! That's good. You're really making progress."

I laughed softly.

"Is that funny?" He looked puzzled.

"No," I said, "it's just that Ralph Thompson was here a little while ago and said the same thing. All of a sudden everyone is an art critic, and everyone can tell that I'm making progress."

Larry looked at me seriously. "You are, you know, and I think you know it too. So why would you resent it if anyone else tells you what you already know?"

I let the matter drop.

"Did you enjoy the morning?" Larry asked, changing the subject.

"Yes, I did," I said. "Though I'm not sure Frank did."

"Poor Frank," said Larry.

What did Larry mean by that? "He's not so poor," I said, annoyed.

"Aha!" said Larry.

"And how about you?" I asked. "Did you enjoy your morning?"

"Yes, I did," Larry said, "but I don't know about Lynnette."

"Poor Lynnette!" I said.

We both laughed then. I put my paint brush down, and Larry moved closer and kissed me warmly.

"I wish you had let me take you to the Olgas," he said. "I could have saved you from sliding down the mountain."

"It was all right," I said, feeling oddly protective toward Frank.

"Well..." Larry said, then he kissed me again.

"Why did you quit climbing when you saw me?" I asked abruptly.

"Why, because I decided I'd rather talk to you than climb a mountain."

Somehow the words didn't ring true. But the conversation was pleasant enough. We enjoyed being together and were surprised to notice after a while that it was getting toward evening.

"Come on, let's go see the sunset," Larry said.

"All right," I said, "but you'll have to help me carry my things."

That night we were doomed to disappointment. The sun set without ever casting a last glow on the rock.

"Well," said Larry, "there's always tomorrow."

"Yes," I said, "but I'm still disappointed. I've learned to love this rock."

"So, you love a rock," said Larry. "Figures."

"What's that supposed to mean?"

"I don't know myself," Larry said, kissing me again in the fading light. "Let's take the bus back. We'll get there sooner and I'm starved. After all, we have all this equipment to carry."

I felt a little disappointed, but I agreed. We piled on the bus and, back at the hotel, Larry helped me carry my things to my room.

"Give me a little time," I said. "I need to freshen up for dinner."

"Right," he said. "I'll meet you at the bar. We'll have a drink before dinner."

I felt very reflective while I was getting ready. I finally decided to just let things take their course. And then I went to the bar. I was afraid Larry might not be there, remembering the first day I had been at the hotel. But he was there, all right, wrapped in serious conversation with Ralph Thompson.

When I arrived, they jumped to their feet.

"Nice to see you again, Melissa," said Ralph. Then he turned to Larry. "I'll see you later. Think about what I said."

"What was that all about?" I asked when he left. Even as I asked, I knew it was none of my business.

And apparently it was not, for Larry brushed it aside. "Oh, nothing," he said. "That Ralph Thompson is a bore."

We had a drink then and Larry talked about the rock, how he had climbed it on just about every side. I realized again how little I knew about him and tried to draw him out. "What kind of work do you do?" I asked.

"I told you the first day you came," he said. "I'm an explorer, an adventurer."

"Yes," I said. "That makes a good hobby, but what do you do for work?"

"Well, you don't think exploring can be work?" Clearly he didn't want to tell me.

"I know you're American," I said. "Where were you born?"

"I was born in a log cabin in the hills of Kentucky," he said.

"Oh, Larry, you're impossible!"

He talked about inconsequential things, and then we moved into the dining room. Supper was fun. Larry talked about some of his adventures. He had been in many parts of Australia.

"Have you ever gone to Coober Pedy?" I asked.

Larry looked at me strangely. "Yes," he said finally.

"I've been there. I even went down into the opal mines. Very interesting but such a godforsaken place."

"You like mines?"

"To look at. I wouldn't like to work in one." Then he asked, "Say, how about you and I having an adventure? Tomorrow we'll go out in the Land Rover. I promise not to do anything to scare you or put you in jeopardy. And," he added, raising his hand, "I promise to bring you back before the day is over, safe and sound. OK?"

I looked at him and laughed. "All right," I said. "I'll go with you."

That evening Larry and I took a walk about the hotel. Everything was quiet and dark. There were a few sounds from the room where the slides were shown. "Let's see the slides," Larry suggested. "It's the closest thing they have here to going to the movies."

"All right," I said. "I saw them when Colin showed them. Even if they are the same ones, they're very good."

They were exactly the same slides, and the young man who showed them was almost silent. And yet, this time the rock seemed so much more beautiful to me. It was as if in the short time I had been here, I had gotten to know the rock as a friend. But there was something disturbing in the back of my mind that I couldn't quite grasp.

When the slides were over, I told Larry I wanted to turn in early. He walked me to my room and said good night.

"See you tomorrow morning, right after breakfast," he said. "Or better yet, before sunrise. We could go over to the rock together in the Rover."

I nodded. "That would be fine."

He kissed me warmly and then left. I went into my room and started to get ready for bed, but I felt restless. There were too many conflicting emotions running through me.

Save them, I said to myself. They can wait. Right now I need to sleep. But when I finally fell asleep I did not rest well. Somewhere there was a deep sense of foreboding, of disaster, just beyond the range of my consciousness.

CHAPTER XIV

I awoke the next day to the sound of knocking on my door. I sat up, alert and frightened, and called out, "Who is it?"

"It's me, Larry. Time to get up and get ready to see the sunrise."

"Already?" I shouted, glancing at my watch.

Even as I said it, I knew that he was right. I would have to hurry if I wanted to see the dawn. I jumped out of bed, hurried into my clothes, and opened the door. Larry was standing there.

"Thanks for waiting," I said, pulling my sweater around me against the chill.

"It will warm up," he said, taking my arm. "Come, let's get in the car and go over to see the sunrise."

In a few minutes we were huddling together on the hillside facing the huge hulk of the rock.

"There it is!" he said, as the first rays of the sun appeared directly on the rock. I didn't answer. I didn't want anything or anybody to disturb the early silence, the morning mating of the sun and the rock.

91

Dawn was beautiful, as if the sun was making up for the neglect of the evening before. It seemed to caress the rock with yellows and golds. And then it was over. The whole earth now shared in the warmth and the light. Day had begun.

"Have you really been getting up every morning for the dawn?" Larry asked, as we headed back to the hotel.

"Well, just about every morning. Remember, I came here just to appreciate the rock."

"No excuses necessary," Larry said. "To each his own."

"But you like the sun too," I pursued.

"Yes," said Larry somewhat thoughtfully. "But I don't worship it or the rock the way you do."

"I guess I could be called a sun worshipper." We both laughed then as we reached the hotel. We ate quickly, so we could soon start on our adventure. I was excited about going out for the day. All the apprehension I had felt the night before was pushed to the back of my consciousness.

"Is there anything I need to take along?" I asked, as we left the dining room.

"No," he said. "Just yourself, lovely lady."

Soon we were on our way. We took a dirt road that led away from Ayers Rock, in a direction I had never gone.

"We could get lost out here," I said.

"Yes," said Larry, "and don't think it hasn't happened. The old-timers tell many tales about people who went out into the wilderness and never came back."

"What do you think happened? They got lost and starved?"

"Yes," said Larry, "but apparently, some went wild

with apprehension and did foolish things. One man shot himself because he was lost and felt hopeless. The irony was that when they found him he was only about two miles from a road."

"Oh." I shuddered. "Please don't tell me any more tales like that."

"I won't," he said, "and I won't do anything foolish like that. I have too much living to do."

We passed over uneven ground and after a while, I was sure that we were no longer on a road. In the distance I could see Mt. Olga, but it was receding. All the land was amazingly similar, rugged, flat, with spinifex and gnarled scrub trees.

"It's so much alike," I said. "I would think it would be hard to establish landmarks."

"That's right," Larry agreed, "but watch the sun. You can see that we're now traveling west. We won't stay out at night, but when I do I watch the stars. You know, don't you, that we can't see the North Star here in the Southern Hemisphere? Here we use the Southern Cross as a point of direction."

"That's interesting," I said. "So you are something of a navigator."

"I have to be," he said, "in my line of work." He looked at me, laughing. I opened my mouth to ask about his work, but he interrupted me.

"This is supposed to be a fun day, an exploring day," he said. "I don't want your puritan ethic to interfere with us."

"All right," I said, "but tell me about your exploring."

"Right now," he said, "*we* are going to do some exploring." He stopped the car, motioning for me to remain quiet, and we got out. I followed him over to a hill. When I caught up with him, he pointed ahead.

"There's an aborigine settlement," he said, "but don't let them see you."

Ahead of us was a low valley, with some white trees.

"Those are called ghost gum trees," Larry said. "They're a sign of life, because you can always find a little water wherever they are, if you dig deep enough."

There were people in the valley, aborigines dressed in ragged clothes, sitting on the ground, and I stopped when I saw them. Larry looked back and saw that I wasn't following him.

"Come on."

"No." I shook my head. "I don't want to bother them."

Larry smiled at me. Then he walked back and said, "Listen, I should have explained. These aborigines are my friends. I always play a little game with them. I try to see if I can sneak up on them without their seeing me. I've never succeeded."

"Oh," I said. "Well, that explains it. I thought you were spying on them."

Larry took my hand, and we went over to the group. The three people—two men and a woman—sitting on the ground turned and looked at us. The younger man jumped up and went over to Larry.

"Larry!" he shouted.

"Rudolph!" Larry took his hand. "It is good to see you. And how is Mary and little Kin?"

At the mention of their names, Mary smiled up at him. Little Kin looked out from the lean-to.

"They are all very good, very good," Rudolph said.

"This is Melissa," Larry said, pointing at me. They all looked at me carefully.

"OK," grunted Rudolph, smiling broadly.

The older man, with a scarred and wrinkled face, got up and went over to Larry. "Whiskey," he said. "Do you have whiskey?"

I was taken aback, but Larry was not fazed.

"No," he said, "no whiskey."

"Whiskey," the man said sadly. Then he said, "Cigarettes? Do you have cigarettes?"

"No cigarettes, no whiskey," said Larry, holding his hands open.

The old aborigine turned away, losing interest. Rudolph looked at Larry and shrugged.

"Well," said Larry, "I guess we'll go and try to surprise you the next time."

Rudolph laughed. Mary and Kin laughed too, in imitation.

"Good-bye," said Larry.

"Good-bye," they all echoed.

We were nearly back at the car before we started to talk. "Rudolph is the only one who can speak English," Larry said. "Mary and the child do not understand the language at all."

"That older man," I said. "He could speak a little English. Wasn't he pitiful?"

"Well," said Larry, "for better or worse, that's how some of the aborigines are these days. They've lost their own heritage and the only parts of the white heritage they've accepted are the vices."

"Just like the American Indians," I mused.

"Well," Larry went on "there are others like Rudolph who have retained much of their heritage. But they can hardly survive."

"So it's integrate with the white culture," I said. "Surely there should be another way."

"Listen," he said, "I don't know much about anthropology but this I do know. When one culture meets another one, the weaker one will disappear unless it adopts the ways of the stronger."

"And then it disappears too," I said.

"Melissa," he said, "you feel sorry for those aborigines, and I love you for your compassion. But feeling sorry never helped anyone. I'm sure there is no easy solution to their problems."

We drove on then, seeing again more spinifex. Here and there we saw small trees.

"So there is some water under the soil," I said. "Why don't the farmers here irrigate and use this for farm or pasture land?"

"It's been tried," Larry said, "but it wasn't successful. Along with water under the surface, there are apparently huge layers of salt. And when these were brought to the surface, they made things worse than before."

"Another problem to solve," I said, sighing. "And another problem. This weather!"

Larry laughed. "I will excuse that," he said, "because you're new in Australia. But it gets very hot here at this time of the year. There have been years when the temperature stayed over a hundred for weeks at a time. As a matter of fact, this is a nice day. But the evenings are still often chilly.

"How about some lunch?" he asked. "I told you I'm well prepared for anything. Peanut butter sandwiches?"

"Peanut butter!"

"Nothing better," he said. "I see a good place ahead. Just where those ghost gums are. This soft land is really a stream we're in. But there's no water unless there's a pouring rain. And if there is, we'd better watch out."

"Really? I can hardly believe that. This whole area is so dry."

"They tell me that when flash floods come, they destroy everything in their path."

"Well," I said, "let's hope that they stay away for a while. At least until we finish our peanut butter sandwiches."

They were delicious. Larry brought out some cold drinks from his ice chest and we had a good lunch. Afterward we sat there for a while holding hands.

"I've looked forward to taking you out," he said. "It's too bad you said no the first time."

"Yes, but it didn't seem to bother you too much. You had Lynnette."

Larry shrugged, started to say something, then apparently changed his mind. He put his arms around me and kissed me. Soon we were locked in a warm, tender embrace.

Suddenly Larry let out a howl. I jerked away from him. "What's the matter?"

He was howling and jumping. "I've been bitten!" he shouted.

And then I saw the culprit. A snake was slithering away. "What kind of snake is that?"

"A brown snake," said Larry. "It's poisonous! Here, take this knife and cut the bite open."

I took the knife and stared at it. Larry was moaning with pain.

"All right," he said angrily, "I'll do it myself. You'll have to suck on it to try to get the poison out."

He took the knife and with a quick cut opened the wound between the fang marks.

I bent over him and began sucking on the wound, spitting out the blood.

"I think that's enough," Larry said finally. He was terribly pale. "Now give it another slice with the knife so the fresh blood will wash it out."

After I did that, Larry said, "Now help me back to the car. I have some snakebite medicine you can give me."

He leaned heavily on me as we got into the car, all the time moaning softly. I found the medicine and gave him some. Then he slouched in the seat.

"You'll have to drive," he said. "Take the keys." Then he slouched over, asleep.

CHAPTER XV

Terrified, I looked at Larry, so white, so drained. All the while, he was moaning ever so softly. I knew we had to get help, so I turned the car around and headed in the direction that I thought was right. But how could I know? I regretted deeply that I had paid so little attention to the way we were going.

Still, I had a good sense of direction. But with each mile, my doubts grew. Was this really the way we had come?

Larry slept on. I looked over at him, thought of waking him, then changed my mind. If worse came to worst, we could spend the night in the Rover. We would probably be safe. Larry had brought enough food and water.

I saw occasional ghost gum trees, but their silhouettes all looked alike. I was not sure whether or not we had passed them before. If only there was some kind of landmark.

The only one I could think of was the valley where we had seen the aborigines. But where were they now?

And then I noticed with a pang that the gasoline was low. Surely Larry had an extra supply somewhere. We had to find a road! I stopped the car and woke Larry, gently shaking his shoulder.

"What?" he said groggily. "What are you stopping here for?"

"Larry," I said, "how does that bite feel? Are you better?"

"It's very painful," he said. He pulled up his pants leg and looked at the wound.

"But we're in luck, so far. There doesn't seem to be any redness around it. Maybe you did manage to get all the poison out."

"Larry," I said, "I'm glad about that. But I'm worried about us. I've been driving two hours now and I haven't the slighest idea where I'm going. I haven't even seen any signs that I recognize. Every rock, every ghost gum, and especially every spinifex looks alike to me. And to top it off, it looks like we're running out of gas."

Larry looked at me and then he smiled. "It's not all that bad," he said. "I've often gotten lost out here. Let's take our bearings."

He squinted at the sun. By my watch it was about twenty minutes after three.

"Well," he said, "by the sun you are headed east, which is the right direction. But we didn't come exactly west, as you know." He got up then and tried to get out of the car. He stretched out gingerly, favoring his right leg, then he quickly sat down again.

"I'm weaker than I thought I was," he said. "I guess it takes all the body's resources to fight out enemies like snake venom."

"Just stay sitting," I said. "I'll be glad to drive. But first tell me where you keep a spare can of gasoline."

Larry told me where to look and soon I was filling the tank, glad that it was there, even happy with the smell. We needed that gas if we were going to survive.

"Do you want anything to eat?" I asked.

"Not right now," Larry said. "We'd do better to save our food."

At that I felt a chill running through me.

I drove on and on. And not once did I see anything I could recognize. Larry sat hunched in the seat, not talking, just watching the land with careful eyes. At last he turned to me.

"We would have been back at the rock by now if we were going in the right direction," he said. "But we can't even see either Ayers Rock or Mt. Olga."

"What shall we do?" I asked, very frightened.

"I don't know," he said. "Just keep going, I guess, because nobody is going to come looking for us. At least not yet. But, if you don't mind, I'm going to sleep. I can barely keep my eyes open. This snakebite medicine does that."

I drove on, fighting panic every minute. And then I thought I saw a low valley with some white gum trees. The aborigine settlement!

I approached with lifting heart. But I was doomed to disappointment. Right where the lean-to should have been were only some low spinifex bushes and some huge spider webs. It was starting to get dark now. I drove faster, just when I should have slowed down. But I was trying to drive away from the worry and panic that threatened to choke me.

The sun would set soon behind me. All I wanted to do was to get back to the rock, back to the hotel. I found myself longing for my quiet little room.

Something made me stop and turn around. I

watched the sun in its full splendor as it covered the desert with its last rays. Then the sky grew redder and dropped lower in the sky, showing up with stark beauty every shrub and ghost gum tree. Then it simply dropped from the sky. It was magnificent.

I felt so much better, so much more able to try to get home. And then the rain began to fall. At first I didn't think too much of it. Then the raindrops began to pelt the windshield in earnest.

I turned on the lights and windshield wipers, but it was very dark. At one point I almost drove into a ghost gum tree. I tried to wake Larry, but he just moaned. I wasn't sure what to do. Should I drive to some higher ground and stop for the night?

At that, I realized with a flash the meaning of the ghost gum I had nearly run into and why I seemed to be following a trail. I was in a river bottom. If this rain continued, it would turn into a mighty river.

And then the wheels began to clog in the mud.

I did the worst possible thing. I panicked. I hit the gas with full force and drove myself deeper into the mud.

"Larry," I shouted, shaking him vigorously. "We're going to drown!"

Larry opened his eyes and looked at me blankly. "What's the matter?"

"We're in the mud and I can't get out! We're in a river bottom! We're going to get stuck when this turns into a river!"

Larry looked at me blankly again, shook his head, then reached over and took my hand again.

"Relax, Melissa," he said very gently. "It's all right. Now, please tell me once more what you just said. And say it slower."

I took a deep breath. Then I tried again. Larry started to laugh. I looked at him, hurt.

"I'm not laughing at you," he assured me. "I'm just laughing at our situation. One man bitten by snake while kissing. Sweet girl forced to spend the night with said man because she gets car stuck in the mud in the desert."

He laughed harder. I looked at him, slowly melting. Then I laughed too. But not for long. "Larry, what should we do?" I asked.

"Well," he said, "stop spinning your wheels."

"OK," I said. "Then what?"

"Now get out and see if you can find any logs or anything to put under the wheels. I'll try to help you if I can."

"No, Larry," I said, "just stay there. Don't try to help unless it becomes a matter of life or death. But please stay awake. I need your support."

I got out and started to look around. Finally I found a log sticking out from some mud. I pulled on it, but it didn't budge. I pulled again, in short, quick pulls, trying to shield myself from the rain. And then, I remembered. Stop, I said to myself. Relax your shoulders and try again, with firm determination. And the log slowly began to move.

It took a great deal of effort to pull the log over to the car and try to wedge it under the wheel. Larry was holding the flashlight for me as I worked. Finally I got it there.

"Now you got one," he said. "I think if you get another log that size for the other front wheel we can make it. But I'm going to help you, snakebite or not. I can't bear to sit and watch you."

Together in the rain, we found a log even bigger than

the first one. We pulled it over to the car and shoved it under. Then Larry sat down, breathing heavily.

"Are you all right?" I asked.

"Yes," he said. "I just need to get my breath."

"What should I do now?" I asked, feeling weak and helpless.

"Just find a few more little pieces to push around the edges."

It took me some time to find them as very little wood was available in the desert. At last I thought I had the car all set.

"Now," said Larry, "you stay out there and watch. I'll try to drive the car out of this mess."

He moved to the wheel with great effort. Then, with full determination, he got the car started. The wheels spun for a moment until they took hold of the logs. Then with a whine and a rasp of the engine Larry had the car out of the mud.

He carefully maneuvered the car up the sloping sides of the river bottom. I ran behind him, then he stopped the car and let me in.

"I wasn't trying to keep you wet," he said. "I thought I might need you to push. Now drive a little way from this stream until you're on high ground. There we'll spend the night. There's no way we can go on."

I drove the car slowly and carefully. It was an eerie feeling, seeing almost nothing and not knowing where the highest ground might be. But I realized that I was slowly pulling uphill because of the pull of the engine and the way the lights shone.

Larry sat beside me apparently too exhausted to talk.

"This is good enough," he said at last.

I stopped the car and turned to him. "Tell me what I

can do for you," I said. "You're so weak. What can I give you?"

"Well," he said, "I think we should eat something. And we should get into some dry clothes. No sense catching pneumonia in the desert. I have some old clothes somewhere in the back, jeans and shirts and stuff like that. I hope you don't mind."

"Fine," I said, wiping the water off my face and arms. "I'm cold and chilled to the bone with this rain."

I went into the back and found the clothes. A little later we had both changed. We didn't look like fashion models, but at least we were dry.

Larry looked at me and laughed. "You're beautiful," he said. "Melissa, do you realize that this is the first time I've ever seen you in hippie clothes? And you look beautiful. Wet, stringy hair and all."

"You look pretty good yourself," I said, although he seemed exhausted. "And now for supper." I handed him the sandwiches I had prepared.

"What would we do without peanut butter?" he asked.

After we had eaten I felt extremely tired. "I'm ready to think about sleeping," I said.

"Me, too," said Larry. "One of us can sleep across this front seat and the other can stretch out in the back. Which do you choose?"

"I don't know," I said, "but since you're the sick one, I think you'd better take this cushioned seat."

He looked at me sheepishly. "I hate to be sick," he said, "but I like all the attention it gives me."

At that we kissed good night and I climbed into the back. I was asleep in no time.

But I awoke a few hours later, my back aching from the hard surface. I sat up carefully, not wanting to wake

Larry, and looked around. There he was, peacefully sleeping. His handsome face shone in the moonlight. And I realized then that the rain must have stopped.

I looked out the window. The moon shone on the dark and empty world. It was completely quiet except for a few insects. What a strange country. I really didn't know anything about it. I don't even know anything about Larry, I thought. But I do know that he needed me today, and even though I got lost and got us stuck in the mud, he needed me as much as I needed him.

CHAPTER XVI

Morning dawned beautifully. I was awake to watch it. Dawn on the desert was very different from dawn near the rock. Here there was no special colossus to focus on, no special display expected. As a consequence, the sun covered and warmed the whole world equally. At first there was only golden light covering the earth, then the full yellow arrived, and then it was day. No doubt about it. And it would be warm.

I looked around. Larry was still asleep, his face showing a good color. I decided not to wake him just yet. Instcad, I quietly slipped out of the Rover and took a little walk. There was precious little evidence of last night's rain. I wandered down to where the ghost gums were and found the still muddy tracks of our car from last night.

I smiled to myself. That flood never did come. I guess I overestimated. Oh, well, what an adventure it was!

l looked around a little longer at the beautiful morning, all the freshness of a new world. How strange, I

107

thought. Australia is supposedly the oldest continent on earth but it is the last to be inhabited by the industrialized world. Here in the Great Outback, it has all the newness of a new creation.

I wandered back to the Land Rover. Larry was sitting up in the front watching me. "Good morning, beautiful," he said.

"Good morning, Larry," I smiled at him. "How's that bite this morning?"

"Take a look," he said. He pulled up his pants leg. The bite was somewhat swollen, but there were no terrifying red marks leading away from it.

"Is it better?" I asked. "Still looks puffy."

"I think so," he said, "but I won't feel happy about it until we get to a doctor. However, I feel so much better today that I'm anxious to get moving."

We ate breakfast then, fresh fruit and canned rations from his supplies. We even managed to boil a billy and have some instant coffee.

"Of course," said Larry, "we're not doing this right. In the old days this would have been tea. The old-timers would always heat a pot of water and throw in their tea."

"Sounds good," I said, "but I'll take coffee any day."

When we had finished eating, Larry said, "Let's get going. We may be a lot closer to home than we thought."

And he was right. We set out in the morning sun and after we had traveled about half an hour I thought I saw something.

"Hey, hey!" I shouted. "Isn't that something?"

Larry laughed. "Well, it certainly is something. And from right here, I think it has a good chance of being Ayers Rock."

It was more to the north than either of us had

thought. Now that we were within sight of safety, we both became very talkative.

"What an adventure!" I said. "But all's well that ends well. When you don't know what to say, use a cliche. That's what I always say."

We both laughed over the triple rhyme. Then Larry said, a little more seriously, "I just want to see a doctor about this bite. Then I'll be all right."

We took our time driving now. We even stopped to eat some lunch. "Wouldn't it be something," I said, "if something happened now and we were in sight of the rock and we couldn't get there? That's the kind of thing that happens in bad dreams."

"Yes," said Larry. "I've had bad dreams like that myself. That someday I'll find what I really want out of life and I won't be able to get it when it is in sight."

I was silent, wanting to ask more. But Larry turned to me. "Melissa," he said, "what do you want out of life? Do you know?"

"I want to paint," I said.

"You want to paint," Larry repeated slowly. "I notice you don't say you want to be a great painter. Is painting itself the thing you want or do you hope to achieve success?"

"I guess I never thought about it in those terms," I said. "I've always known that I wanted to paint. And I want to be a good painter, so that I can think of myself as a painter. And others can think of me that way. But I guess that's not possible without some kind of success and acclaim. And in art there is only one way that is achieved. Are people willing to pay good money to buy one of my paintings?"

"So," said Larry, "it all boils down to financial success."

"I never thought about it that way before," I said,

"because money is not what I want."

"No," he said, "I don't think it is." He was silent for a while. Then he asked, "But really, Melissa, is that all you want out of life?"

"No," I said. "I guess not. I want to be someone special to someone."

He was silent again. How difficult it is for men to show their feelings, I thought. They have a hard time coming to terms with their feelings, much less talking about them.

"So you're going to marry someday," Larry finally said.

"Well," I said, trying to lighten the mood, "they say that about ninety-six percent of all Americans marry sometime or other."

"Yes," said Larry. "There are times when I think it will happen to me too."

"Oh, come on," I said "They say that marriage is what most men need and want; they get more benefit out of it than women do."

"Well," he said, "that all depends on who the men and women are."

At that he was silent and so was I. And then we hit upon a road.

"Civilization at last!" Larry shouted. And our conversation stayed on superficial levels after that.

We arrived back at the hotel, dusty and tired. After being out all night, lost and snakebitten, somehow I imagined there would be people running out to meet us. But the people walking around the grounds of the hotel barely noticed.

"Nobody even knew we were gone," Larry said.

"Too bad," I said. "I felt we were some kind of heroes, and nobody even notices."

We parked the Rover and went into the hotel to ask for a doctor. There was one available on the grounds and he saw Larry within a few minutes. I waited while Larry was being checked by the doctor. In a little while he called for me.

"This doctor is going to give me an injection," Larry said, "and it hurts already. I need you, Melissa, to hold my hand."

I held his hand and Larry exaggerated the pain of the shot. But it was pleasant being with him.

"I have good news for you," said the doctor. "I think you're going to be all right. Just be careful for the next few days. Come back to me if there is the slightest change in the wound."

"I'll do that," Larry said, and then we went back to the Rover to clean out our things.

"Here," said Larry. "Why don't you just take your things? I'll help you carry them. You should go to your room and get some sleep."

"Sounds like a good idea," I said.

A little later I was in my room. I showered slowly, enjoying the spray of warm water all over my body, getting rid of all the grime, all the tension of the previous day. Then I lay down to sleep a little, though I didn't think I would be able to. But the next thing I knew there was a knock at the door.

I looked at my watch. It was late afternoon. I had slept for several hours.

"Who is it?" I called.

"Frank. I came to see if you were all right. I hadn't seen you around."

I got up and went over to the door. "I'm all right," I said. "I just got back today. We went out in the Outback and got lost and stuck in the mud."

"We?" he asked.

"Yes," I said. "I went with Larry."

"Oh," said Frank. He was quiet a moment. "Well, if you want a ride, I'm going over to the rock to see the sunset now."

I thought of Frank, standing sadly outside my room, and said, "OK. I'll be ready in a few minutes."

Frank smiled warmly at me as I opened the door. "I was worried about you when I noticed that you weren't here for sunset last night nor for the sunrise this morning," he said.

"Thank you for worrying," I said. "It's good to be back safe. We did have quite an adventure."

The drive to the rock was short. "Why are you driving?" I asked. "I thought you preferred to walk."

"I was afraid you might be sick or something. I was going to offer to drive you over in my car to save you from walking. And then it got too late and we had to drive if we wanted to get there at all."

I was touched by his consideration.

The sunset at the rock was different this night, full of purples and ochers, not at all the gold it had been in the morning.

"I never cease to marvel," I said, "at the way the sunset is different every day. How can nature keep coming up with new ideas?"

"Well," Frank said as he moved closer, "nature does wonders. You are a wonder of nature too. And I want to tell you again how glad I am that you are back."

When we got back to the hotel, the receptionist called out to me. "You're Melissa Carrington, aren't you?"

"Yes."

"Catherine has been asking for you all day."

"OK," I said. "I'll go right to her. Thank you."

Frank came with me. Catherine was sitting quietly in a corner, seemingly in quiet contemplation.

"Melissa," she said, extending her hands, "how was the sunset tonight?"

"Very different," I said. "A very purple sunset. It's the only one of that kind I've seen yet."

"I worried so about you yesterday," Catherine said. "You were in great danger."

She looked directly at me, with those strange unseeing eyes. "Weren't you?"

"Well," I said, "it seemed so at the time. But here we are, all safe and sound back at the hotel."

"Melissa, Melissa," she said. "Be careful. You always misunderstand me. I am not speaking of the kind of danger you are. Think what I mean. You are always able to get yourself out of a lost trail in the desert, or a falling rock, or even down a mountain."

I frowned. "What do you mean, Catherine?"

Again Catherine focused all her power on me. "I'm quite sure you know exactly what I mean," she said solemnly.

CHAPTER XVII

The evening passed quietly. Frank and I talked a little after supper, but we both seemed to be hedging. I could sense Frank's depression. It was infectious, and soon I felt depressed too.

"Well," I said, "I'm ready to call it a day. In spite of sleeping all afternoon, I'm still very tired. So, Frank, thanks for everything. But now I am going to bed."

"All right," he said. "I understand. I'll walk you to your room."

We walked slowly, almost silently. At the door to my room Frank gave me a quick, soft kiss.

"Good night." I said.

"Good night."

I undressed slowly and went to bed, feeling extremely sad. What was wrong? I didn't know. But one thing I knew for sure was that I needed time to work out all my feelings. Too much had happened in the last few days for me to be able to cope with it all.

I fell asleep, only to waken in the middle of the night

with a strange sense of fear. Something in the back of my consciousness worked through to disturb me.

Colin! I was thinking of Colin.

"He did not die a natural death," Catherine had said.

I was no longer able to sleep. I lay there in the darkness, not wanting to think. All I wanted to do was live through the next few days and paint.

All I want to do is paint, I said to myself. No that's not all. That's all I wanted to do when I had nowhere else to turn. That thought was even worse. Now sleep was utterly impossible, so I got up, turned on a light, and looked at my canvases, one by one.

There was no doubt about it. Each canvas I had done was better than the previous one. And suddenly I knew that I would be able to paint well today.

I pulled out my paints and started on a new painting; a sunrise. I worked in the sky and the background, with fleeting glimpses of color, the foreshadowing of the dawn. A few clouds, low and flattened, awaited the coming of the sun.

I sketched the dark stubble, a shadowy tree, and then the rock. And then it was time to go out and see the sunrise.

The morning was gray and chill. I walked quietly over to the rock, all alone.

As much as I feared and suffered with loneliness, I liked solitude, I liked being with my thoughts, in the early morning, I didn't want anyone to break in and disturb my communing with myself.

But now I realized that I was not alone. There was someone coming after me. "Wait," Ralph shouted. "I'll walk you over."

I turned. I was disappointed, but there was no gracious way I could refuse.

I stopped and waited. He joined me, huffing and puffing from his rapid walk.

"I told you," he said. "It's too dangerous to walk over here by yourself."

"Yes, I know," I said. "You told me. But what do you really think could happen? Are there a lot of crooks who hang around at the rock?"

"No," he said, "but there is a lot more danger here than you think."

"Why are people always trying to scare me?" I asked. "Catherine is always giving me prophecies of doom."

"Well," said Ralph, "if she says it, it must be true. You'd better listen to her. But I'd rather talk about you right now. I missed you yesterday. I heard that you were out with Larry."

"Yes," I said. "We had a good time."

"I'm sure," said Ralph. "Did he show you any of his secret haunts?"

"His secret haunts?"

"Yes," said Ralph. "You know he takes a lot of girls out in his car. Did he give you that old ploy about being lost, so you'd have to spend the night out there?"

"What?" I asked.

"Oh, come on," said Ralph. "You know how Larry is."

"No," I said. "Tell me."

"My dear Melissa," he said, "it's refreshing to meet one so inexperienced and naive. Larry is the kind of guy that formerly would have been called a ladies' man. He knows how to charm the fair sex; he manages to win over every girl who is attractive. But underneath it all, as the psychologists say, lies a deep contempt for women. But surely you knew all that."

I did not answer.

"Well," said Ralph, looking at me, "I guess I've disturbed you. If I did, I'm sorry. I didn't mean to."

You meant to, I said to myself.

And then we were at the rock. The dawn was subdued. Somehow the clouds interfered too much, and the sun never did get a chance to make a spectacular display.

"That was a disappointment," said Ralph.

But I was not unhappy. As I watched the dawn, I was thinking how I could paint the sun's hesitancy.

"I think I'll take the bus back," I said. "I'm anxious to get back to my painting. I started one this morning before dawn and now I know exactly how I can finish it."

We got on the bus just as it was about to leave.

"Why, good morning," Lynnette said. "How was your day with our dear Larry yesterday?"

"It was OK," I said, without enthusiasm. I turned to look out the window.

But Lynnette was not to be put off. "Wait a minute," she said. "I'd like to join you if I may."

She moved over to sit with me. What could I say?

"So when do you plan to go out with Larry again?" she asked.

"I have no plans," I said.

"No plans," she repeated. "I'm surprised. But I'm sure you'd be able to change all that. What did you and Larry do all day?" she asked. "Do you want to hear what Larry and I did?"

"No!" I said. Then I stopped and looked at her. "Lynnette, what's the matter? Why are you so angry with me?"

Lynnette looked at me and then went back to the other seat. I sat there, feeling miserable.

When we got back to the hotel, I decided to skip breakfast. Everyone that I had talked with so far had irritated me. I decided I'd keep away from everyone. Just take my easel and go back to the rock.

It was a relief to be going off again. This time no one called after me, no one bothered me. The morning was quiet and chilly, but I knew it would soon be quiet and warm. I nibbled on some crackers as I went.

I set up my easel not far from where we had seen the morning sunrise. It was broad daylight now but in my mind I had a very clear image of what the sun had been like this morning, the disappointing, not-quite-achieved sunrise, which blossomed into full day none-theless.

I went directly to work. As you work on a painting, it seems to take over itself. Suddenly it achieves its own identity and there is only one way that it can be completed.

After several hours, I stepped back. What I had just painted was good, very good. Not great perhaps, but very good. And then I realized that I was hungry.

Well, I said to myself, you've worked hard this morning. Now you deserve some time off and something to eat. That's enough painting for the day.

My depressed mood of the morning was over too. This morning I had wanted to avoid everyone, but now with the full sun and a feeling of satisfaction in my painting, I wanted to talk. I wanted to eat lunch in the dining room with some people I knew.

But I was doomed to disappointment. I met no one that I knew on my way back to the hotel. There were a few new tourists around, mostly native Australians, a few Americans, some Japanese.

We nodded and smiled briefly to each other. I found

a place at one of the tables in the dining room and tried to keep up my end of a strained conversation with two couples from   Perth. And then Doreen, Sylvia, and Georgia came in. They saw me at once.

"Melissa!" they shouted. "We're back!"

"So I see," I said.

They pulled up chairs around me, ignoring completely the two couples. The Australians soon left and the three girls clustered around me, telling me all that they had seen and done since they left Ayers Rock.

"We went down into the opal mines," Georgia said. "They were neat. It's a great place to visit, but I wouldn't want to live there."

She laughed heartily at her own joke.

"What have you been doing, Melissa?" asked Sylvia. "Painting?"

"Yes," I said, "I've been painting. And I think I'm getting better."

"Great," said Georgia. "Let us see a picture sometime, will you?"

"Yes," I said softly. "Sometime."

Doreen turned to me, serious now. "Is Larry still here?"

"Yes," I said. "I think so. At least he was here yesterday."

All three girls breathed a sigh of relief.

"Well, girls," I said, feeling like a maiden aunt, "you know that all three of you can't have Larry."

"Why not?" asked Sylvia, laughing. "At least we'll give him a choice. But we're willing to share him three ways."

"Just three?" I asked.

They looked at me. "Is Lynnette still here?"

I nodded.

"I wish she would go," said Doreen. "Maybe we can tempt her with a trip to the opal mines. Why don't we give her an opal and tell her to go and get some more?"

"Well," said Georgia, "let's go find him."

I finished my coffee slowly and went out of the dining room. This was my day to explore more of the rock. And I guess it would have to be alone. Well, I thought, I did have some company at lunch. What more could one ask for than three girls like Doreen, Sylvia and Georgia all at once?

I walked slowly back to the rock, passing the side where many tourists were trying to climb. One day I had climbed it. One day with Larry I had reached the top. What about Larry?

I moved on and entered a little cave not far from the climbing area. It was empty and did not look like it had ever been used for anything. But of course it had. Through the centuries all these caves had been used. In hard times they had sheltered people. It was sobering to imagine what it must have been like in those long-ago times, living in a cave in the side of the rock that was supposed to be sacred.

Again I moved on. I was near the aborigine compound. I approached it slowly, not wanting to offend anyone. Did aborigines still use it much? Were any there now? From what I had understood, it was a ceremonial cave, used only a few times a year when the aborigines were inducting young men into manhood.

As I pondered this thought, I looked up and saw Larry coming down the side of the rock. He slowly lowered himself into the compound.

CHAPTER XVIII

I watched Larry for a while. I stepped back out of his sight, because for some reason I didn't want him to know I was there. He clearly wanted to be sure that no one was watching him. He looked around carefully once he was in the compound, in my direction, beyond the fence.

He knew he was breaking a law by entering the compound. That was restricted area, a sort of reservation that white people were not to set foot on.

Apparently satisfied that there was no one watching, Larry entered the cave and was lost to my sight. He emerged in a few moments, carrying a small brown bag that he slipped into his pocket. Then he moved deeper into the compound, where I could not see him.

Apparently he climbed out another way, for I did not see him again. I stood there a long time wondering what had just happened.

What had Larry taken from the compound? Or had he brought the sack with him? Why was he being so secretive?

I was deeply disturbed, more at my own attitude than at Larry's odd behavior. After all, I was the one who had hid, who had spied on him, and it was just the day after I had spent a day with him.

It was my own feelings that I was concerned about.

I moved out of my hiding place and started to look around further to take my mind off things. My feelings were too much for me to handle just then.

I came to Maggie Springs, which was rather deep after the recent rain. The water was clear and cast a reflection, and it would have been beautiful under other circumstances. But all I could think of was Colin, who had died there. Had he too just come from the aborigine compound? Had he just seen something that meant something—that he was not meant to see?

It was too much. I was relieved when the three girls showed up.

"Melissa," Georgia asked, "have you seen Larry?"

"I think he's around the rock somewhere."

"We need him!" Sylvia said.

"Who do you need?" asked a male voice.

"Larry!" all three girls shouted at once. And they went off with him. He looked at me before he went, with a strange look in his eye. It looked like he was apologizing. But for what? Surely I didn't resent it that he wanted to go off with the girls. Or did I?

Frank arrived soon and I was happy to see him. Was Maggie Springs the meeting place at the rock? If you waited there long enough, perhaps sooner or later everyone you knew would come along.

"Hello, Melissa," he said quietly. "It's good to see you. How has your painting gone this morning?"

"Very well," I said. "I worked all morning and I was so pleased with my work that I decided to take the afternoon off and see some more of the sights at the rock."

"May I accompany you?" Frank asked. "Or would you rather be alone?"

"No," I said. "I was alone all morning. I'd be happy to have you with me."

"Have you seen the kangeroos' take yet?" he asked.

"Is that that piece of rock that seems to just hang on the edge?" I asked.

"Yes. Have you had a chance to see it close up?"

"No, I haven't, but I'm sure that it has a special meaning to the aborigines."

Frank laughed softly. "Yes," he said, "everything meant something. It was their sacred pole turned to stone."

"Like a totem pole?"

"Definitely," said Frank. "Or at least we think so. We still know so little about the aborigines. They lived in a real world, a fierce world of many enemies— warring tribes, harsh weather, in constant danger from their environment and from wild animals—but they compensated for it by a world view composed of dreams. They thought that the world was peopled with many invisible people who became visible only in dreams. In dreams they could return to previous lives, to a time when life was different."

"Frank," I said, "have you talked much to aborigines?"

"Not nearly as much as I would have liked," he said. "It's so difficult to get them to be themselves when I am there, so difficult to get them to say what they really feel rather than what they think I want to hear. They're living on the edge of a powerful civilization and in this day and age it is necessary for them to depend on us.

Unfortunate as it may be, it's true, and the aborigines know it. So as a consequence they want to please us, and they try to give me answers that they think I'll like."

"That's too bad. But what's the solution? Go live with them for a while?"

"Yes," said Frank. "That's the only way. And I'm planning to do so soon. But I'm just not ready yet. There's another problem I must solve first. Remember my colleague who fell from the mountain?"

I nodded and he went on. "Paul Morrison. He didn't fall. I am more and more sure that he was pushed. And I'm beginning to think that I know why and who did it."

"Frank," I said, "are you saying that he was murdered?"

"I don't like to use that word," he said, "but it wasn't an accident."

"Why would someone kill your colleague?"

"For money," he said bitterly. "Why else? People usually only kill for love or money. And I don't think the man who killed him knows how to love."

"Frank," I said, "what do you mean, money? Does it have anything to do with opals?"

"Yes," he said, "but not in the way you think. Those uncut opals are practically worthless. No, it's not that. But I think it has a lot to do with opals."

"You're being very mysterious."

"Yes," said Frank, smiling briefly. "But for your own safety I can't be anything else." He changed the subject then and I was glad. He was making me more uncomfortable even than I had been. We talked a while about how Ayers Rock meant so much to the aborigines.

"There's talk about building a lot of modern conveniences here. Like establishing a huge airport for daily trips, a resort hotel..." Frank said sadly.

"Oh, no," I said. "That would be terrible."

Frank nodded. "And I just found out that the Australian government itself has hired a professional American tourist firm to work out some plans for all this. It's as if they figured that our country would be the one to know how to turn a natural wonder into a national pollution disaster."

"It makes me sick," I said. "But do you think they will really do it?"

"That all depends on how much they think they need the money. And it also depends on what the average Australian citizen feels about it."

"Hmm," I said. "From what I've seen, Australians aren't much better than we are about preserving the environment."

We wandered to other sites, and finally Frank said, "Let's walk a distance from the rock so that we can look at the broad side."

"Is that to see that brain they talk about?" I asked.

"Yes," Frank said, "but you know for sure that that must be the word of the white man. The aborigines didn't concern themselves with interior anatomy."

From a distance, one part of the rock looked exactly like a brain.

"All those little crevices meant something to the aborigines," Frank said.

"Part of the escape route of the carpet snake people from the venomous snakes?"

"Yes," said Frank, "part of the bloody legend. The stories of the aborigines are full of blood, but that is the kind of harsh life they had learned to cope with."

"And yet," I said, "they certainly didn't destroy the land. They lived here for a long time and there's little evidence of it. They lived in harmony with the land instead of feeling that they had to control it.

"And that's an interesting concept," I continued, "because it happens in painting too."

"You mean you try to work in harmony with your painting?"

"Precisely," I said, "and that reminds me. I just thought of another painting I could do. I think I could cope with this brain erosion on this side of the rock."

"Let's look at the stage," said Frank, "before you get too carried away with the brain. I think the stage will inspire you too. In my opinion it's one of the strangest sights at this whole rock."

The stage was a sort of hollowed-out cave that looked like a huge inverted wave, about seven feet from the base. It was as if millions of years ago this area stood next to the sea and the huge waves came and left their imprint. How strange it was to realize that the rock was inland, thousands of miles from any sea.

"This is fantastic," I marveled as I stood in the corner of the cave looking out.

"Yes," said Frank. "The acoustics are wonderful here. That's why they call it a stage."

"Marvelous," I said, in my booming voice.

"And just think," said Frank. "When they set up this place like a resort town they'll make this an outdoor theater. Maybe put on plays of aborigines and Australians."

"Oh, Frank," I said, laughing.

He came over to me and kissed me then, standing under the wave effect. I felt happy in his arms.

"Come," said Frank. "Let's walk around some more. I know another cave."

It was not far. We climbed up the piles of rocks and soon we were far inside the cave. There were a few rabbits scampering around there, but other than them, we were alone.

"You weren't afraid to climb this time," Frank observed.

"No," I said. "I didn't even think of fear."

"Good," said Frank. "I was afraid that after the time at Mt. Olga, you wouldn't want to climb again."

"No," I said. "I think that's all over."

We went down in a little while so we wouldn't miss the sunset. Tonight it was worth seeing, full of brilliant colors.

"I just never get tired of that sunset," I said with a sigh.

"Neither do I," he said. "It's as if nature plans all day to give us a brilliant finale."

The evening passed quickly. Frank and I ate supper together. I saw Larry enter the dining room with Lynnette later, but I barely glanced in his direction.

After supper I showed Frank my paintings.

"You're doing very well," he said.

"Thank you," I said. "But I'm my own worst and best critic. I do think I'm getting better, and I'm quite pleased about it."

When it was time to go, Frank kissed me again. "Good night, Melissa," he said. "I enjoyed the afternoon with you tremendously."

"I did too," I said. "I'll see you tomorrow."

I slept well enough that night, but in the morning I awoke with the distinct feeling that something was wrong. Then I realized that I had overslept and missed the sunrise.

Annoyed, I got dressed and went to breakfast. Lynnette met me at the door.

"Good morning," she said. "Well, how do you feel today?"

"Fine, thank you," I said.

"I'm surprised," she said.

"Why?"

"After the quarrel you and Frank had?" she asked, in a mocking tone.

"We didn't quarrel," I replied.

"No?" she said. "Then why did Frank leave here early this morning in such a big hurry?"

CHAPTER XIX

I was devastated. Frank gone without saying a word? I had to find out more, so I went over to the receptionist. "Has Frank Hanson checked out?"

She eyed me curiously. "Why is everyone so worried about Frank today? You're the second person to ask. As far as I know he's coming back. He didn't officially check out. We're still holding his room."

"Someone else asked?" I prompted.

"Yes," she said, but apparently she had no intention of telling me who, so I thanked her and left.

I took my paints and wandered over to the rock. By now the sun was high in the sky. I was disoriented, as if not getting up to see the sunrise was like not eating breakfast or brushing my teeth. The day had started without me and now I had trouble fitting in.

I went back to the north side to see the brain again. In the morning light it was not attractive. Indeed, the entire rock looked forbidding this morning. Had I offended it by not being present for the morning ritual?

Such nonsense, I said to myself. Enough of this. If I

let myself go long enough, I could convince myself that the rock was some kind of living being.

I set up my easel and pulled out my paints. Well, the rock as a living entity was not a bad idea. And I might as well paint it with its brain.

I was soon engrossed in my work. Before long I was very warm. Again I had forgotten how warm the days were under a blue sky that was unbroken by clouds. The rock seemed to stare at me as I painted, like a haughty and noble person who was sitting for a portrait. Suddenly I realized that I had worked straight through lunch. I was hungry but not ready to stop. In my painting, the hulk of the rock seemed like a strong person. You could count on it if it was your friend, but otherwise . . . And right now I had the uncanny feeling that I didn't know whether or not the rock was my friend.

I didn't dare offend the rock further. I ignored my complaining stomach and painted on.

And finally the painting was finished. I was very pleased. The rock stared out at me, and now I felt a peace with it.

I left the painting to dry in the sun and went up closer to the rock. When I got there, I sat down in the shade and pulled out some crackers I had brought with me. Not much of a lunch, but it would hold me until supper.

I relaxed in the shade. After a while, I put my head back and closed my eyes for an instant. A little rest won't hurt me, I thought.

But I must have fallen asleep, for how long, I had no idea. The next thing I knew, I was awakened by the sound of voices. One was Larry's. He was quite near me by this time, though I could not see him.

"Don't bug me!" he said. "Just give me time."

Someone answered something in a low, calm voice, then Larry shouted, "Don't push me too far. I don't frighten easily, and I have no intention of letting you mess things up for me."

I stood up and looked in the direction of the voices. Over the scrubby bushes I could see Larry's fair hair glowing in the sunlight. And then I knew who the other man was—Ralph Thompson. What was going on with those two? This was the second time I had heard them quarrel.

They were moving away from me now, over to the other side of the rock. I got up. stretched my stiff muscles, and headed back to my easel.

My painting was dry now. My mother had been right, I thought happily. She knew that Ayers Rock would be a source of inspiration for me.

But then why was I so disturbed, so uneasy? I seemed to be unable to find contentment here. During my stay at the rock I had felt so frightened, so distraught about all the things that had happened, so unsure of my own emotions for both Larry and Frank. I had thought inspiration was a peace-giving thing that would come when I was calm. But I had not known much calm here.

I was worried about Larry. He was so strange to me. He blew hot and cold. I could never be sure whether he liked me or not. And then there was the competition. I was more disturbed than I cared to admit that he had so many girls hanging on him.

And then what about Frank?

I picked up my easel and paints and told myself, Go watch the sunset and see if you can end the day any better than you started it.

It took me a while to walk over to the west side to face the rock as it accepted its last caresses from the sun. There was already quite a crowd there, brought in by the tourist buses.

Always the tourists, I thought, and then I remembered Frank's horrible predictions of things to come.

I hope this area never gets built up, I thought, yet I knew I would never have seen the rock if some accommodations hadn't been provided for tourists. Typical, I thought. Everyone wants to go, but he wants to be the last one in and keep everyone else out.

The sunset was gentle tonight. It was as if after a full day, the sun was tired. The rock, which all day had been somewhat harsh, now shone with a soft yellow. It almost looked as if it were of some kind of soft material, warm and loving to the touch. I felt warmed inside by it. I had been in my usual place, all alone, watching the sunset, when I became aware of someone approaching me. I turned. It was Lynnette.

"I see you have your own private place to see the sunset," she said. "You don't care to join the rest of the tourists on Sunset Strip."

"Well," I said, "it's not that so much. It's just that I enjoy watching the sunset in silence."

She laughed a little, then she turned serious. "Melissa," she said, "it's very important that I talk to you. There are some things we have to get straightened out."

"All right," I said, looking her straight in the eye. "What do you want to discuss?"

"Oh, no," she said. "Not now. Let's go to supper and then meet afterward. Will my room be all right?"

She told me her room number and I agreed to meet her there later. She steadfastly refused to give me even a hint of what she wanted to talk about. I was full of apprehension. In a way, I felt the way I used to feel when I was summoned to a principal's office. Why did Lynnette have this effect on me?

I knew why. Compared to her, I was dead. Her whole being was alive. She glinted with excitement in the way she walked, talked and thought. To her, I was a quiet stick-in-the-mud. But apparently she took me seriously.

I left supper early for I had no desire to prolong the agony. Before I left, I took a quick look around the dining room. I did not see Lynnette at all during the meal, and she wasn't there now. Had she skipped supper altogether? Or hadn't she arrived yet?

I decided to go directly to her room and get this confrontation over with. I found her room easily. She was situated in the newest wing, the most modern accommodations. She answered my knock immediately. "Come in, Melissa," she said, "and sit down. This crummy hotel has only two chairs, neither of which is comfortable, but you can sit on the bed if you want."

I sat down in one of the chairs and looked at her, waiting.

"Look," she said. "I'm not a person to mince words or hold grudges. But I want to get some things straightened out with you. OK?"

"Well," I said, "if you tell me what you want to get straightened out, I'll think about it."

She grimaced. "OK. In simple words, it's Larry. Keep your hands off him, and stop influencing him!"

I looked at her for a while. Then I said softly, "Lynnette, it's not a matter of getting my hands off him. Larry does what he wants."

"Yes," Lynnette said, "but with your sweet innocence and painting, you're getting him all mixed up. He didn't used to be like that. Before he met you."

"Oh," I said, "I didn't know that you knew him previously. I thought you had just met him."

Lynnette laughed bitterly. "No," she said. "We were engaged for a while. But we reached a point where we needed to get apart to see if we were ready to get married. Larry left and came here. I stayed behind. But not for long. I followed him here, hoping he would still be mine, because now I know I want him. And you're here!"

I protested. "I'm sorry. I didn't know. But even if I had known, that wouldn't change anything. Larry has to do his thing. You'll never win him by trying to tie him down."

Lynnette went on, scarcely listening to me. "He's mine. He's always been attracted to any pretty girl. And they always like him. That's why I don't mind when the three teeny-boppers, Doreen and company, chase after him. I know Larry better than that. He enjoys them but they will never mean anything to him. But you are different. It's your seriousness that attracts him. Larry has never met anyone like you."

I didn't know what to say. It was clear that Lynnette was suffering. But deep within me somewhere was a feeling of satisfaction. I did mean something to him!

She looked at me, almost as though reading my thoughts. "There's much more," she said, "that you should know. I don't want you to take Larry away from me because he's mine, but I also think you should be more careful. Larry is into things that are way out of your depth."

"Like what?"

"Like some of his adventures. You're far too puritanical to appreciate them."

"Thanks," I said, "but I don't appreciate being called puritanical. This is the first time we've talked. What do you really know about me?"

"More than you think. And certainly more than you know about Larry. You didn't know he was engaged. But then, he might have been married for all you know about him."

She was right. But by now I was angry. "Is there anything else you wanted to say?"

"No, that's it," she said. "Just keep away from Larry."

I did not slam the door when I left, but I was not gentle with it. When I got to my room I sat for a long time staring at the wall. Well, Lynnette was certainly right about one thing. I knew almost nothing about Larry.

I was still sitting there when there was a knock on the door.

"Who is it?"

"Larry. Melissa, I have to talk to you."

Well! If Larry wanted to talk to me, that was fine, Lynnette or no Lynnette. Later when I had time to think about that evening, I realized that Lynnette had influenced me to go with Larry. To get back at her, I was trying to be more adventurous than usual.

"Oh, good," Larry said as I opened the door. "You're not going to bed yet."

"No," I said. "It's still fairly early."

"Good. Melissa, I need you. Can you go out to the rock with me?"

"Now?"

"Yes," he said, taking my arm. "I need your help out at the rock tonight."

CHAPTER XX

I hesitated. Something deep within me was warning me that to go out to the rock at this time of night was dangerous. But Larry was coaxing me.

"Melissa," he repeated, "I need you."

"All right," I said, pulling on a sweater and getting ready to go.

"Good." Larry gave me a little kiss, took my arm, and we were on the way.

"Tell me what this is all about," I said.

"Well," said Larry, "it's rather complicated. But you'll see when we get there. I'm going to try something tonight and I want someone to be there to help me if I need help. Let's call it a secret mission."

"I'm not sure that I like secret missions."

Larry laughed softly. "I guess I *am* sounding mysterious. I just need someone with me that I can trust. And you're the only one that I can."

"Well," I said, "that's flattering. But how true is it? What about Lynnette?"

139

Larry slowed his steps and looked at me. "Lynnette? Why do you bring her up?"

"Larry," I said, "she told me that you two were engaged. Or still are, or something."

He was silent for a little while. Then he spoke slowly. "Let's just say that Lynnette and I were once engaged. Period. No comment on the present or the future."

I had more to ask but I hesitated.

"Has she been bugging you?" he asked

"Well," I said, "we only spoke a few times and she is always angry with me. She wants me to keep my hands off you. I told her that my hands weren't on you."

Larry laughed a low, somewhat bitter laugh. "Ah, so she's jealous! I like my women that way."

I felt a chill.

By now we were getting closer to the rock. It glowed in the moonlight. "The rock is beautiful tonight, isn't it?"

"Yes," said Larry, "it looks so soft now. During the day it always seems so hard."

"And you ought to know," I said. "All the climbing you do."

"Yes," said Larry, "climbing is just one of my things. But I'm going to do only a little climbing tonight. And I might as well tell you about it now. I'm going to climb into the aborigine compound. I'd like to have you near to act as sort of a lookout."

"Why are you going into the compound? Isn't that illegal?"

"Yes," he said with a soft laugh, "but not much more illegal than walking on the grass or jaywalking is. A good reason is enough."

"And you have a good reason?"

"Yes," Larry said, "but I can't tell you. You'll just have to trust me."

I was silent. I just didn't know whether or not I really trusted him.

"Here," he said. "Try this." He pulled a small whistle from his pocket. When I blew it, it made a low, cricketlike sound.

"What is it?"

"Just a special whistle," he said. "You can use it if anyone approaches the compound while I'm in there. I'll hear it. They will too but they'll just think it's a natural sound."

"I hope so," I said. "I'm not sure I like the idea."

"Listen," said Larry. "I appreciate your helping me, and I assure you that you're not in any danger whatever. Even if someone wanted to hurt me, they wouldn't hurt you."

"What if a Park Ranger comes?"

"They won't," Larry said. "They never bother going out to the rock at night."

We arrived at the aborigine compound then, and Larry looked around carefully. He checked out the bushes around the compound, the nearby caves. The bright moon lit up the surface everywhere, but the shadows looked even more forbidding.

"All right," he said. "Now you stand over there near the rock. That way you'll be able to see anyone who approaches from this side. If anyone comes, blow on that whistle. Just a few short, quick blows. Be sure to stay hidden."

"I don't think I like this," I repeated. "If it's someone I know and like can I come out and talk to him?"

"No," said Larry. "Nobody. Just stay hidden."

We looked at each other for a while. Then Larry put his arms around me and spoke very softly to me. "Melissa, I know I'm asking a lot of you. But please, trust me. I trust you. You're the only person at the hotel that I trusted enough to ask to come here."

"All right," I said. "Just don't stay in long. I won't feel good about all this until you're out."

"Hopefully, nobody will come," Larry said. "I just have to be sure." He kissed me then, a warm and tender kiss. Then he climbed over the fence and into the compound.

He was soon out of sight, slipping back into the shadows near the rock. I moved over close to the rock and looked around. Then I slipped in behind a bush where I was sure, with the shadows and the dark, that no one would see me. But I had a good view out. I could see anyone who might approach, because the fence to the compound was in the open moonlight.

Time passed slowly and no one was near. Then the world became perceptibly darker. The moon had slipped behind a cloud.

Suddenly I heard a very soft sound. Yes, there was someone approaching. I squinted my eyes to get a better look. Was I imagining it?

I strained my eyes. I thought I saw a dark figure near the fence. Just then the moon came out from behind the clouds and I could see clearly. A man was standing by the fence, his back toward me. He was dressed all in black. I put the whistle to my lips and blew a few short puffs.

The man stopped and didn't move a muscle. He looked my way. Although I was sure that he could not see me, I was petrified. And then he started to walk toward me. Now I could see his face. Ralph!

I was too frightened to move. I could not even tremble. I did not blow the whistle again. I just stood there, hoping that Larry had heard it the first time.

Then Ralph stopped in midstep, he turned, and moved away, out of the area. Had he been frightened away? Or was he only leaving and circling back to see what would happen?

I pushed closer to the rock so I could not be caught from behind. I stood there for what seemed an eternity, and then I saw Larry come over the compound's fence. He didn't seem to be carrying anything. He moved quietly, with a smoothness that did not betray either fear or awareness of danger.

He stood near the fence after he had climbed over, looking around in all directions, peering into the darkness in the far distance. Then he came over to where I was hiding.

"Melissa," he whispered. "Are you here?"

"Yes," I said softly, coming out. "I'm glad to see you."

"So there was someone here?" he asked.

"Yes," I said. "Larry, it was Ralph. Larry, what is this all about? I've had enough of your mystery. Ralph is not my dearest friend, but at least he is an acquaintance. One that I have nothing against. But now, apparently he is dangerous."

"Keep your voice down," Larry said urgently. "I'm sure he is still around."

"Tell me what this is all about," I said again, speaking softly now.

"I will," Larry said. "As soon as I can. But I can't tell you right now." He stopped speaking then and we were both aware of the sounds of someone approaching.

Ralph stepped out of the shadows, holding a gun. Both Larry and I were taken aback.

"Ralph!" said Larry. "You come at me with a gun?"

"Yes," said Ralph, "but I certainly have no desire to hurt you or Melissa. All you have to do is give me what you got from the cave."

"But I haven't taken anything from the cave."

"We'll see," said Ralph. "Spread your hands on the rock and let's do a search."

Larry looked at him without moving. I knew he was calculating. But then he said, surprisingly, "OK. But let's let Melissa get out of here. This thing has nothing to do with her."

Ralph met Larry's eye and then he nodded. "OK," he said. "She can go. This has nothing to do with her. Melissa, get out of here. Get back to the hotel. Don't come back. Don't worry, Larry and I will work this out. One way or another."

I looked at Larry. "Go!" he said urgently.

I left, hurrying away as fast as I could in the darkness. And then I heard a gunshot. I had to go back. I approached the area slowly, terrified. I was picturing Ralph standing over Larry's body, the gun smoking. Then I pictured Larry standing over Ralph's bleeding body.

When I reached the area where I had left them, I saw no one. Neither Larry nor Ralph. I stood there, silent, trying to listen for sounds. They couldn't be far.

But I was all alone. I walked around the area, trying to see if either of them was nearby. No luck. All I could hear were my own footsteps and the wild pounding of my heart. All I could see were the empty spaces where the moon had hollowed out the night and the dark shadows that it hid. I was all alone.

I could not bear it. "Larry!" I called. But my voice seemed incredibly weak, so I tried again. "Larry!"

There was no answer. I heard an echo bounce off the rock. I tried again. "Larry!"

Still no answer.

I had to take the chance. "Ralph!" My voice was trembling now. "Ralph!" Again all I heard were echoes.

I hurried back to the hotel, looking over my shoulder every few minutes, racing faster and faster, frightening myself with my own wild thoughts.

When I reached the hotel, I went straight to the receptionist. She seemed bored and barely raised her eyes from the magazine she was reading.

"Please," I said breathlessly. "I have to talk to somebody, some kind of police or somebody."

She finally looked at me. "What's happened?"

"I think there's been a murder."

"A murder? You mean, there's a body lying around?" She was incredulous.

"No," I said. "That's what's funny. There's no body."

She looked at me a while, shook her head, and then said, "You'd better start over."

"All right," I said, finally catching my breath. "I was just out by the rock with Larry O'Brien and Ralph Thompson. They were quarreling and Ralph had a gun. I heard a gunshot but saw no one around when I went to look, no one dead or alive."

She looked at me as if measuring my story. "All right," she said finally. "I guess we should call Mr. Harrison. He's the chief security officer around here."

CHAPTER XXI

And then Larry walked in.

"Larry!" I shouted.

He looked at me nonchalantly. "Why, Melissa, what's all the excitement about?"

"I—I was just about to report you as killed."

Larry looked at me hard, then he forced a laugh. "I'm all right," he said. "As you can see."

The receptionist was watching both of us, puzzled. Finally she said, "Listen, you two, Melissa just reported that you were killed, Larry. And now here you are. What happened? Is anyone in danger? Is anyone dead?"

Larry laughed again. "No," he said. "I'm all right. Mr. Thompson wouldn't hurt me. I managed to calm him down. He had no intention of hurting me."

The receptionist looked at me. I hesitated. She asked, "Are you satisfied? Or do you still want to call the police?"

"Where is Mr. Thompson now?" I asked.

"He's probably in his room," Larry said, "or in the bar. I don't keep track of him."

"I think I'll go see him," I said.

"OK," said Larry. "I'll go with you."

The receptionist looked at us again. Then she smiled a little in relief. "Melissa, come back and tell me if there is any problem."

"Larry, what happened out there? I was afraid you were killed. Or he was."

Larry took my arm. "Listen," he said. "As you can see, I'm all right. Ralph didn't hurt me. I should have known you would run back and report it."

"But Larry, I was worried about you."

He softened. Then he smiled and said, "It's all right. I understand. You did it for me."

We were walking by the bar. "I'm going to see if Ralph is here," I said. He was not. Larry waited until I came out.

"So you don't trust me," he said. "You think he came to some harm."

"I don't know," I said. "I have to see."

"So, go see," he said angrily as he left.

Would I see him again soon? I wondered. I wanted to but I was deeply disturbed about what was going on. Well, I said to myself, I'm not going to stand here and wait. I know Larry is all right. I'm going to find Ralph.

But I immediately realized that I didn't know Ralph's room number.

Back to the poor receptionist, I thought. But before I got there, I saw someone else. Catherine was wheeling her wheelchair in my direction. I approached her.

"It's Melissa," she said in her gentle voice. "Come here, child."

I walked up to her obediently. She took my hand, held it for a while, then looked at me with her unseeing eyes.

"Melissa," she said, "you are upset."

"Yes," I said. "I'm worried. I don't know what I want or don't want any more."

"Yes, you do," she said, "if you would just listen to your heart. You are too afraid of too many things. But in your heart you always know the right way to act, the right way to be."

"Do I? Oh, Catherine, why is it that ever since I came to the rock I've been upset?"

"Melissa," she said, "I knew it would be like that for you. Ayers Rock has many things to teach people who are willing to listen. And you are one of them."

"What should I do?" I asked. "Catherine, I don't even trust people I think I love."

"Is it trust or love that you are concerned about?"

"I don't know."

"Yes, you do," said Catherine. "You know so much more than you think you do."

After thanking her I turned to go. Then I turned back. I had one more question.

"Catherine," I said. "You said you didn't think that Colin's death was a natural one. What do you think happened? Was he murdered? Is there a murderer here at the rock?"

Catherine spoke very quietly. "That's exactly what I think," she said. "And you may already know who the murderer is."

I went into the lobby to find the receptionist again, to find out Ralph's room number. But before I did, I saw Frank walking into the lobby.

"Frank," I said, "I'm so glad to see you."

"I'm sorry I didn't tell you I was leaving," he said. "I couldn't tell anyone. I had to take care of something. But I'm back and I'm glad to see you."

We smiled at each other, then Frank took my hand. "Look, let's go somewhere and talk."

"I'd like to," I said, "but first, I have to see what happened to Ralph Thompson."

"Ralph Thompson," Frank echoed, greatly puzzled.

As I approached the receptionist, she smiled at me. "Any murders?" she said lightly.

"I don't know yet," I said. "What is the room number for Mr. Thompson?"

She consulted her list. "Room eighty-five."

"Let's go," I said.

But there was no answer to our knock on Ralph's door.

"Melissa," Frank said, "he's not there. Now please tell me what this is all about."

I told him the whole story, describing exactly how Ralph had pulled a gun on Larry and Larry's attitude later. But Frank was just shaking his head.

"What's the matter with that Larry?" he asked. "Dragging you into a mess like that. Come on, we've got to go back. There's more to this than meets the eye."

"Frank," I said, "it's almost midnight. Do you mean you want to go out to the rock again?"

"Yes," he said, "we have to. If you don't want to come with me, that's all right. I don't blame you. But I'm going out there."

"I'm going too," I said. "But maybe we ought to call security."

"Not yet," Frank said slowly. "This is something I

have to delve into first myself. And," he added, trying to make light of the situation, "there may be no problem at all."

And so for the second time that night I went out to the rock with a companion who was acting mysterious. By now it was very dark and very late. I was quite frightened. Every shadow in the light of the moon seemed threatening. Every sound made me jump.

Frank took my arm. "Melissa," he said, "I know how frightened you are. If you want, I'll take you to your room first and come back alone."

"No, Frank," I said. "It's all right. I'll see what there is to see. I won't be able to rest until I know what happened to Ralph."

"All right, but tell me if you change your mind. I don't want you to go through all kinds of agony. I'd appreciate it if you show me exactly where all this fighting took place."

"All right," I said, pulling my sweater closer around me. It was getting very chilly. I never failed to be amazed how the evenings were, so cool and different from the days. The sun was god in Australia and when it was gone, so was all warmth and life.

Not all life, I thought. At least I hope not. I realized then that I really believed we would find Ralph dead.

I walked around the rock until we came to the aborigine compound. No one was there. Frank looked at me and pulled out his flashlight.

"I'm going to do some exploring in some of the caves and undergrowth here," he said. "You just wait here. Why don't you sit on the large rock over there where you will be visible in the full light of the moon. I'd like to be able to look out and see that you're still safe."

"All right," I said, "but you better be careful. I don't

like the idea of you crawling around in those caves in the dark."

Frank laughed softly. "I'll be all right," he said, "but it's nice of you to care about what happens to me."

I sat there on the rock watching Frank until he disappeared under the bushes. He seemed to be swallowed up in a large shadow. But I never took my eyes off where he disappeared. Occasionally I would see the flickering light of the flashlight coming through the bushes.

Suddenly I heard a voice near me.

"So you are here!"

I jumped. "Larry!"

Larry looked at me, his eyes unreadable. "What are you doing out here?"

"I could ask you the same thing," I said.

"I asked first."

"OK," I said. "Ralph wasn't in his room, so we're looking for clues."

"We?"

"Yes," I said.

"You and Frank, I suppose. I heard he was back today."

"Yes."

"So, where is dear Frank?"

"Around."

Just then I saw a flicker of light from the bushes. Larry saw it too. "So there your friend is," he said. "I guess I'll give him some help."

"I'll tell him you're coming," I said. "Frank! Frank!"

There was a movement in the dark bushes and then Frank appeared. "What's the matter, Melissa?" he shouted.

"Larry's here."

Larry walked over to him. "Yes, Frank," he said. "I'm here. And I'm going to help you."

Frank answered something that I did not hear, and then the two men disappeared into the bushes. For a while I heard some low murmuring, then all was quiet, except for a few night sounds. After a while I got cold and stiff sitting there, so I stood on the rock, then walked around for a while. I was cold, I was frightened, I was tired. I wanted Larry or Frank or both to come back. I did not like being out there alone.

But time passed and I did not hear a sound. What had happened? What if Larry really was a killer and he and Frank had fought? But then I remembered that Ralph had pulled the gun on Larry. What did Larry have that Ralph could want?

And then someone emerged from the shadows. It was Larry. My heart skipped a beat. Where was Frank? And then I saw Frank emerging too. They walked over to me. Larry was the first to arrive. "There was nothing there," said Larry.

Frank said nothing. Larry turned to him. "Are you satisfied?" he asked.

"I guess so," Frank muttered, but he looked far from satisfied.

"Well, that's that," I said. "Let's go back to the hotel."

The two men walked me back to the hotel in silence. Larry left us at the entrance to the hotel, and Frank walked me to my room.

"What was all that about?" I asked.

"Not much," Frank said. "I guess Ralph really is all right. I suspect we'll see him tomorrow."

"Frank," I said, "please tell me what's going on. First I think there is a murder and then people tell me that it's all right. Including you, who seemed to have been afraid of a murder too."

Frank kissed me. "I'm sorry I took you out there tonight," he said. "It was a terrible and frightening thing to do. But go to sleep now. Everything isn't over, but it will be soon. Lock your door when you get in and don't open it for anyone. Anyone! This is going to be an important night and I want you safe."

"Frank, please don't be so mysterious," I said. "Are you going to be safe?"

"Oh, yes," Frank said, obviously trying to be casual. "Don't worry. But now you get to bed."

I went to bed, all right, after carefully locking my door and my windows. But I knew I would not be able to sleep.

CHAPTER XXII

There was never a night like that one. I rolled over and over, unable to sleep. I looked at my watch from time to time. Television would have given me something to dull my mind, but there was no television here. I tried to read but I could not keep my mind on the few books I had.

At last I got up. There was only one thing to do: paint.

I set up my easel, pulled out my paints, and started. This time I just let the paints take over. I painted a wild, vicious scene of the rock. It looked like some kind of monster. The curving lines below it were like a snake. The sky above was full of warning and danger. I painted faster and faster, filling every inch of the canvas, letting the painting grow by itself.

Finally I stopped, exhausted, and stepped back to look at my painting. This was my masterpiece.

I washed my face and hands and lay on the bed. In just a few minutes I was asleep. The terrors of the night had passed through me onto the canvas. The dawn

155

broke and still I slept. I missed another sunrise at the rock.

So did many others, I found out later. Frank was not there, Larry was not there, Lynnette was not there, and there was no way that Ralph could have been there.

I finally awoke to the sound of the maid knocking on my door. I jumped up, frightened. It took me a while to figure out where I was and why it was so late.

"Come in," I called to the maid, as I threw on some clothes. "Come in."

She entered the room with her broom, mops, and other equipment.

"I was afraid you might be sick," she said. "This is the first time I've come that you were still asleep. You're one of my early risers."

"Yes," I said, "but I had a rather sleepless night. I didn't get to sleep until early morning."

The maid then noticed the painting. She started, then she stared at it for a while.

"Did you paint this last night?" she asked. "It's amazing."

"Yes," I said. "I worked at it most of the night."

"It's marvelous," she said. "It looks like you've captured all the fearful legends about the rock."

"It just came out," I said.

"No," she said, "you have gotten in tune with the rock." She leaned forward conspiratorially. "I've lived here at the rock for seven years," she said. "I love this place. But there are times that the rock frightens me, and you've captured that feeling."

"Why, thank you," I said, pleased. "That's what art is all about." I left then and made my way to the dining room to get something to eat. I was starved. The first persons I saw were the giggling trio, Doreen, Sylvia, and Georgia. But they were not giggling today.

"Isn't it terrible?" moaned Sylvia.

"And you were with them," Georgia sighed.

"What do you mean?" I asked.

"You haven't heard!" Doreen said incredulously. "You must be the only one here at the hotel who hasn't!"

"So tell me," I said, feeling weak with anxiety.

"All right," said Sylvia. "Ralph Thompson was found dead this morning out at the rock near the climbing place. He must have tried to climb by himself sometime late yesterday. The security people said he died from a fall."

"And you knew him," moaned Georgia.

"Why would he climb late last night?" Doreen asked. "Surely he knew better than that."

"You say he died from a fall."

"Yes," said Doreen. "He had a huge lump on his head apparently sustained when he fell." It was as if she were quoting official language.

"Oh, my heavens!" I exclaimed.

"And that's not all," Doreen said. "Lots of people seem to have left last night, including Larry."

"Larry left?"

"Yes," said Doreen. "And so did Frank."

"And so did Lynnette."

"And you knew them all," Georgia moaned.

"So did everyone else!" I said.

"But you were special," Sylvia said.

"Come on, let's eat," said Doreen.

During lunch, the girls chatted on about the tragedy. It was difficult for me to ascertain whether or not the biggest tragedy to them was the departure of the men and Lynnette or the death of Ralph. I asked one question.

"Doreen," I said, "when you said that Lynnette and Frank and Larry all left today, do you mean permanently or what?"

"I don't know," she said. "I tried to ask the receptionist, but she said that she wouldn't tell me. I guess she thought it was none of my business."

"Which it isn't," murmured Georgia.

"It is too," said Doreen. "Whatever Larry does is our business."

I left the dining room soon after, to call the security personnel. The receptionist looked at me over her magazine.

"Do you know something the rest of us don't know?" she asked, apparently now interested.

"I don't know," I said. "I just want to talk to security. Will you please tell me where I can find the chief officer?"

"Well, he's busy right now out at the site with the officials. But you're welcome to wait here for him or go out to find him."

"Thank you," I said. "I think I'll try to find him." As I walked out of the lobby, I heard a wheelchair. Catherine was coming my way.

"Is it Melissa?" she asked.

"Yes," I said. "Catherine, something terrible has happened."

"Yes. I knew it was coming."

"What can we do?"

"Is there anything you should do?" she asked.

"Catherine, I am so afraid."

"I know why you are afraid," Catherine said. "You

are afraid that someone you love is something less than honorable. Perhaps even a murderer."

"Yes," I said simply.

Catherine took my hand. "It will be all right," she said, "just as soon as you know who you really love."

"That's just the trouble."

It took me a while to walk over to the rock. There was too much on my mind, too much I didn't understand. And I guess I wanted to be sure that I would not have to see Ralph's body.

Ralph was dead. Colin was dead. Both of them had died from "accidents." I did not believe that Colin's death was an accident, but even more strongly I did not believe that Ralph's was either. I finally admitted to myself that I thought Larry was the one who had killed him.

But even as I said that to myself, I knew that I loved Larry. With all his faults—he could be so arrogant and maddening and selfish—Larry was also full of life and love, the kind of person who was not content to just be an onlooker. He wanted to live with every fiber of his being. He wanted to try things, to explore. Larry had passion. That was what it was. Larry lived passionately, and I admired him immensely.

I loved him. I wanted to fight Lynnette and every other girl to get him if he wanted me.

Now I knew that it would never be, because I knew that Larry was a killer. And I was on my way to tell the authorities that I almost witnessed the murder.

Where did Frank fit in all of this? Where did Lynnette fit in? Why had they gone? I didn't know. Lynnette's absence made my heart ache, for I feared that she and Larry had gone off together. Were they enjoying the fruits of their game?

When I arrived at the site, a small crowd of on-lookers had gathered. Most of them were talking excit-edly. I recognized some, but others I had never seen before, apparently newly arrived tourists. What an experience for them! Just as they arrive at the rock, a man is found there dead, apparently a climbing acci-dent. I wondered how many in that group would have the nerve to climb the rock now.

I remembered the day that Larry and I had climbed. It had been one of the happiest days of my life. I could still see us there on the rock, kissing, enjoying being together.

I walked over to the official-looking men who were talking near the base of the rock.

"Is the chief security officer here?" I asked.

"I'm the chief officer, James Harrison," one man said, looking at me carefully. He was an older man, nearly bald, wearing heavy glasses. But he had a sense of presence that more than compensated for the infir-mities age bestowed on him. "What can I do for you?"

"My name is Melissa Carrington," I said. "I think I can give you some information about what might have happened to Ralph Thompson."

He looked at me carefully again. "Well," he said, "all right. I'm listening."

"I saw Mr. Thompson yesterday," I began. "Last night. But not here. Larry O'Brien and I were over by the aborigine compound. Ralph arrived and the two men started to argue. Ralph pulled a gun on Larry. Larry told me to get out of there. I did. A little later I heard a gunshot. I hurried back but I couldn't find either of the men. It was early evening and already a little dark. So I hurried back to the hotel, ready to call you. But I didn't because Larry arrived then. He said nothing had happened, that Ralph and he were both all right. I went to Ralph's room but got no answer. Later I came out again with Frank Hanson and tried to find Ralph but could not. And then this morning I heard that Ralph's body had been found."

I said all this in a fast monotone, afraid to vary even my tone for fear that my emotions for Larry would come to light. But now that I had finished, I stopped, not wanting to add any more. Mr. Harrison looked at me unwaveringly. Now he frowned and turned to the other men, who were also watching me.

Then he asked me one question, the one I was afraid he would. "What are you telling me?" he asked. "Are you saying that Larry O'Brien killed Ralph Thompson and then he or someone else dragged his body over here?"

"Yes," I answered. "I guess that's what I'm telling you." I almost whispered the words, they were so hard to get out. "That's how it looks to me."

The men conferred, then Mr. Harrison began to shake his head slowly. "The body shows no evidence of having been dragged," he said. "That, of course, doesn't mean that it wasn't transported here in some other way. But it has no gunshots on it. Thompson did not die from a gun wound. He died from a blow on the head."

The gunshot. It was not what had killed Ralph. Why hadn't I thought of that!

I was already enjoying a deep sense of relief.

"Then Larry didn't kill Ralph," I said, my heart immensely lighter.

"Not so fast," said Mr. Harrison. "After all, we haven't closed the case. I'm very interested in what you have just told us. It might throw light on this subject.

But if your friend Larry killed this man, he didn't shoot him. And Thompson wasn't dragged here."

"I'm glad of that," I said, already regretting that I had even voiced my fears.

"Miss Carrington," said Mr. Harrison, "we're interested in some other things about Thompson. Do you know why he was here at the rock?"

"Well," I said, "he told me he was here on some kind of job, as well as being a tourist."

Harrison shook his head. "Well, he certainly wasn't an ordinary tourist. There's a lot we have to check out. We have some more work to do around here, but we'll want to talk to you again, to see if you can help us figure this all out. I'm afraid that this Thompson, which wasn't his real name, by the way, was involved in some messy business. Later we'll want to know all you can tell us."

Stunned, all I could say was, "OK."

"Just stay around the hotel for a while." he said.

"I'm planning to."

I left then, walking back to the hotel even more slowly than I had come. Now I was completely upset. What was going on? I had just accused the man I loved of murder and found out that another man, a boring tourist, was apparently some kind of criminal.

I went to my room and carefully locked the door, although it was bright daylight. I even pulled down the shades and turned on the light. The whole outside world was frightening to me now. I didn't know just where the danger lurked.

Then there was a knock at my door. "Melissa, are you there?"

It was Frank. I opened the door to him without hesitation.

CHAPTER XXIII

Frank looked worn and wan.

"Oh," I said, "I'm so glad to see you. Where have you been?"

"I've had a lot of things to do," he said. "And now I need to talk to you."

"All right," I said. "Come in."

"No," he said. "Not here. Would you come for a ride with me?"

I looked at him. Usually Frank and I took walks. But in spite of my hesitation, right now I wanted very much to get away from my own thoughts.

"Sure," I said. "Where do you want to go?"

"Anywhere," he said. "It doesn't matter, does it? There's a place not far from here I'd like to have you see. It's an ancient river, perhaps the oldest in all the world. Dry as a bone, of course."

"All right," I said. "Let's go."

During the ride, Frank was strangely silent. It was as if he had forgotten that he had said he wanted to talk to me. I decided to let him tell me when he wanted to.

After riding quite a while, I said, "This river is pretty far."

"Yes," said Frank, "but of course you know by now that all distances are great in Australia. That's the curse of this land. It is also the blessing."

"You mean here one can get away from it all," I said.

"Yes, that's precisely what I mean," Frank said very seriously.

I had never seen him so serious before. At last I could stand it no longer. "Frank," I said, "what's the matter? You're not yourself. You seem so tense and worried. What was it that you wanted to talk about?"

"Look in the back seat."

I looked. "Your luggage?" I asked.

"My luggage."

"Does this mean that you're not going back?" I began to feel a deep pain in my stomach. "But me, I'm going back."

"Are you?"

I almost panicked. I fought to keep my voice under control. "Frank," I said, "please tell me what you mean. You're taking me back to the hotel after we visit the river, aren't you?"

"Let's visit the river first," he said, without looking at me. "And then you'll decide whether or not you want to go back."

I did not answer. Better to wait him out and see what happens at the river.

I huddled in the corner of my seat and waited. Frank said nothing. We had been traveling along the road all this time, meeting only an occasional bus or car. Now we turned onto what seemed to be a side road, but the trail quickly disappeared. However, Frank seemed to know exactly where he was going.

I was afraid. We were off the main road, Frank was in a strange mood, and night was coming.

"We'll see a beautiful sunset out here," said Frank. "You always like the sunset."

"Yes," I said, still hoping against hope that this was all some kind of joke. "But I think I'll miss the rock tonight."

"You may miss the rock," Frank said, "but the rock won't miss you. After all, it has been there for thousands of years and will be there long after you're gone."

There was no answer to that.

Then I spotted some white ghost gum trees in the low rays of the setting sun. "Ghost gums," I said. "We must be near the river."

Frank laughed, a low, humorless laugh. "Yes," he said. "We're right in the bottom of the oldest river," Frank said. "I don't know how that squares with the rivers of Paradise, but that's the story geologists tell."

He stopped the car. "This is where we get out," he said, "and where we tell a few stories ourselves."

I got out of the car, a heavy sense of disaster washing over me.

"All right," I said. "Now, what do you have to tell me?"

"Melissa, I'm sure you already know. I don't have to tell you, do I?"

"What?" I asked, puzzled.

He looked at me. "You mean you don't know?"

"No," I said. "What are you talking about?"

"No," he said slowly. "I guess you don't know. It's so obvious to me that I'm surprised you missed it. But"—

he shrugged—"you'll figure it out in a day or so."

"Frank," I pleaded, "please stop being so mysterious." I tried a little laugh, which came out shaky. "Please tell me what you're talking about."

"All right," he said, "since it's just a matter of time. I guess you know how Ralph died."

"What?"

"I killed him," Frank said, his voice trembling. "Ralph was still out at the rock. I saw him when Larry and I went there. We let him be. After I took you to your room, I went back out. We argued. I killed him. But honestly, Melissa, I didn't mean to. I had no intention of hurting him. He came at me, I pushed him, and he fell. But Melissa, you know me, I'm so weak. How could I kill him? But who will ever believe that it was an accident? I have no life left now. I'm a murderer. I've got to leave. I can't bear to go to prison."

"But Frank," I said, "no one will accuse you of murder. You did it in self-defense. The most you could be accused of is manslaughter."

"Manslaughter is bad enough," he said. "I can't go to prison. All I can do is escape. Run away."

I reached out to him. "Frank," I said, "you know you will solve no problems by running away from them."

"This problem I will. But Melissa, I want to take you with me."

"With you!"

"Yes," he said, his voice shaking—was it with fright or fear of rejection? "Melissa, please come with me."

"I can't, Frank," I said. "I can't."

"Why not?" he said. Then he paused. "Don't answer that," he said slowly. "I know why. You're in love with Larry, aren't you? I knew you were. I was a fool to think that you would ever love me."

"Frank," I said, then I stopped. What should I do, apologize for not loving him? I thought to change the subject.

"What were you and Ralph arguing about? I've had the feeling for a long time that there is an awful lot of shady dealing going on at the rock."

"Sit down," said Frank, motioning to an elevated spot near a ghost gum tree. "I'll tell you what Ralph was up to."

We sat down. I felt cold and very frightened, but I was eager to hear what Frank had to say. I was overcome with sorrow for him, for all that had happened to him. I too felt the heavy burden that was weighing on him. He wanted to confide in me, yet I knew that telling me would not make it easier to bear. Instead, it might just make me a dangerous person.

"You remember I told you once that there was something strange that happened to my friend Paul Morrison, about a year ago?"

"Yes," I said, remembering the story.

"Well," he said, "I've found out what it was all about. Or at least what most of it was about."

"And what was that?"

Frank sighed, his shoulders heaving and then drooping heavily. "It's such a long and complicated story."

Then he started painfully. "Well, it seems that my friend was watching tourists, as I told you. He found them every bit as interesting as aborigines or other pre-industrial people."

He sighed again and seemed to search for words. Finally he continued. "Well, one day as Paul was watching the tourists he saw one that looked different. By now he knew all the different kinds of tourists, those who were genuinely enthralled by the rock, those who were bored with it, those who came here only to be able to write home about it. But one man was acting differently. He was like a man who was trying to escape.

"So Paul followed him, watched him. Everywhere this man went, he carried a huge, heavy satchel. One night Paul saw the man hide the satchel near the rock."

Frank paused. I had to ask the question, "Was that tourist Ralph?"

"Yes," said Frank, "it was Ralph. And the satchel was full of money, as Paul soon discovered. Then he did a reckless thing. He took the satchel and moved it to a different hiding place. And that was his undoing.

"Ralph panicked when he found his satchel gone. But he figured out that Paul, the only person who seemed to be always around, must have moved it. One day he enticed Paul up to the top of the mountain and tried to scare him into revealing where it was hidden. But he went too far. Paul lost his balance and fell."

"Did Paul tell you some of this before he died?"

"Yes," said Frank, "he wrote me a letter. But there was a lot I didn't know. Meanwhile Ralph hunted for that satchel. When he couldn't find it, he hired people to look. Still no luck. Finally, he hired Larry.

"He told Larry that it was a bag containing opals and that it had been stolen by aborigines. He said he didn't want to go to the police because he didn't want to make any trouble for the aborigines.

"Larry was suspicious from the first. He tried a trick, sprinkling a few uncut opals around to see what effect it would have on Ralph. It had an effect all right, as you know."

"So that was the story of the opals," I said.

"But I suspected Ralph of killing Paul," said Frank, "even though Paul hadn't given me the name of the tourist. Finally, last night it came to a head.

"When Larry and I went out there, Larry told me his part in the story and I told him mine. We saw Ralph there, hunting. He saw neither of us. So we just left him there. But I wasn't satisfied. I guess I wanted to be a hero."

He paused again, looking incredibly sad. "When I left your room I went out again to the rock. I found him near the tourist climb. I confronted him. Naturally, he denied everything. I pressured him, even lied to him— told him that I had all kinds of evidence, hoping to scare him or trip him up. But he was not to be disturbed. He laughed at me, told me he would have me arrested for threatening him. I took a swing at him, in the air. What a foolish thing to do! He hit me then. I came back at him and gave him a push. He fell against the rock and hit his head. I expected him to get up and come after me, but he didn't move. He just lay there. Finally, I went up to him, felt his pulse. He was dead."

Frank ended his monologue very quietly, the last words almost inaudible. Then he put his head in his hands.

I felt a deep pain and sorrow for him, and did not know what to say or do.

"I've ruined it," he said, "but I can't go to the police. I can't go to prison. I never meant to hurt him. I only wanted to help my friend."

"Frank," I said, "you're not a murderer. That was an accident."

"Yes," he said. "It was an accident that he was killed.

But it was no accident that I tried to hit him. I swung out at him. I had no idea that killing a human being would be so easy."

He laughed bitterly at his own statement.

There were so many things I did not understand. I wanted to ask more, but Frank looked so pitiful, I couldn't.

"That's why I have to leave here now," he said, "and I want to take you with me. If you don't love me, and I know you don't"—my heart went out to him at the pain reflected in his eyes—"could you at least have a little pity on me? You don't have to stay with me forever, just a little while. I'll understand. And maybe someday you will come to love me, as I love you."

I knew, no matter how sorry I was for him, that I could not accept his love under any circumstances.

"Frank," I said softly. "I can't. You know I can't. And it has nothing to do with Larry. It has to do with you. I can't go along with you because of pity. You know that. And you don't want to spend your life being pitied and not loved."

"I know," Frank said. "I just want you any way I can get you. I love you so."

I shook my head, then reached over to him, touching his hand. "Please, Frank," I said. "Let's go back. Let's go back and talk to the authorities. You'll see, it won't be as bad as you think. You don't want to spend your life as a fugitive."

"No," said Frank, "I'll never go back."

"Please!"

"No. No. And if you won't leave with me, I'll go alone."

He was angry now. I tried to be gentle, knowing how he was suffering. But now he pushed me away angrily.

"I'm leaving," he said. "You'll never see me again."

"Frank!"

"Don't plead with me," he said. "You told me your-self I couldn't stand pity."

He got up, jumped into this car, revved up the engine, and sped off.

I stood there, all alone by the ghost gums, watching the evening shadows.

CHAPTER XXIV

The sunset was fantastic, even better than when it was reflected on the rock. But it would be pitch dark soon, and I would get very cold sleeping out under the stars. Already I wished that I had worn my sweater.

I had to think. I could not stay here. But as long as I could see the ghost gum trees I knew that I was in a river bottom. And I knew which direction Frank had driven from the road. All I had to do right now was try to get back to the road. Maybe someone—anyone— would come by and pick me up.

With the last rays of the sun lighting up the white gum trees, making them look like ghosts in an eerie landscape, I tried to orient myself.

I walked on, as fast as I could without tiring myself. I did not know what else this night held for me, but I had no intention of just lying down and letting things happen. I had to tackle this problem and solve it.

Even as I thought that I realized how much I had changed since I had left the United States. Before, I would have let circumstances take control. But here there was no place to lie down, no place to escape. I had to master the situation.

And then it was completely dark. I could see the moon on the horizon and knew that before long it would rise and the sky would be lighter. But now it was quite dark. I peered up, trying to find the Southern Cross.

Suddenly I saw a light and heard a noise. A bus was fumbling by. Without my knowing it, I had almost stumbled on to the road. There up at the top a bus was just now passing.

"Wait! Stop!" I shouted. The bus rumbled on. I ran after it, shouting all the time. "Please, stop, help me!" But the bus went faster. Soon all I could see were the red tail lights, and then not even those.

I stood by the side of the road and looked a long way. As far as I could see there was only darkness.

I started to walk, since walking would keep me warmer than lying down. I was not in the least bit tired. And as long as I could, I would continue to walk, I decided. That way I would be less likely to miss any car or bus or motorcycle that went by.

I walked on and on. The moon rose, the stars became brighter. It was unfortunate that I was in no mood to appreciate the stars. They were so bright and beautiful, so undimmed by pollution, that I should have stopped and enjoyed them. But all I could think of was that I had to get *somewhere*. I had to go where it would be safe. I had to find some shelter for the night.

Deep in my heart I was hoping that Frank would reconsider and come back for me.

Poor Frank. I felt angry with him now, leaving me all alone out here in the Great Outback of Australia, but I felt more pity than anger. Frank was a sad person.

I could not love him; I could only offer him my pity.

And then I knew why no one had loved me. It was a sobering thought. But I also knew that I was no longer that way. In Australia I had become a whole person.

My thoughts turned again to that story Frank told me. I could understand how he felt about prison. But he was making a mistake. And then I thought of someone who would suffer in prison even more than Frank. Larry.

What about Larry? I loved him. I felt a deep sense of relief that Larry was not Ralph's killer. But what had happened at the aborigine compound? Why had Larry gone in there anyway?

My love for Larry was tinged with a sense of uneasiness. When this was all over, I would have to have a long talk with him.

When this was all over.

Larry. Where are you now? I remembered that he too had left the rock. And Lynnette had gone. They had gone together, I felt sure. Was their romance back in shape? My heart ached, and I knew that Lynnette and Larry's departure together caused me more pain than my predicament.

By now I was getting very tired. My feet hurt and burned with the effort, and the backs of my legs were beginning to complain. There was a large rock along the road, and I decided to stop a little while and rest on it. It would have been a beautiful night, if I were not alone and exhausted on a deserted road.

I got up and tried to walk again. But exhaustion took hold, I could no longer get up the speed or the energy. Instead I moved slowly, every step an effort.

A hundred times I looked at my wrist where my watch usually was, but I had not worn it this night. I had no idea what time it was. I couldn't even estimate.

Then I saw a light. A car was approaching. I stood in the center of the road, ready to spring to the side if it didn't see me in time. I waved my arms, shouting.

The car slowed down. The driver must have seen me.

Then I recognized the car. It was Frank's. He had returned for me.

"Come in," he shouted, barely stopping. "Come on."

"Oh, Frank," I breathed my relief. "Thank you for coming back for me."

"Yes," said Frank, with only a wan smile. "I had to come back. I couldn't leave you out there. But I'm not going to take you back to the hotel. We're going as far as we can go, whether you want to or not. The choices for you aren't very good, you know. Either you go with me or you stay out here."

"I'll go with you," I said, all the time my mind racing ahead to think of ways I could get away. After all, Frank had to sleep sometime.

"Good."

"I'm so tired," I said.

"Are you hungry? There's some fruit in a bag on the seat behind you."

I turned around and found the bag. I pulled out some bananas. "Do you want one?" I asked, almost giddy. It was as if we were going on a picnic.

"Yes," he said. "Thank you." We munched bananas in silence.

Then I put my head back and before I knew it I must have fallen asleep. I jerked awake a little later, with a painful neck.

"So you slept," he said.

"Yes," I answered. "You must be tired too."

"I am," said Frank. "Let's both rest a little."

Without further ado, he turned off the main road and pulled onto a side one. He stopped the car and turned to me. "Melissa," he said, "you know how much trouble I'm in. We'll talk about it later. But for now, let's get some sleep."

I nodded. Within minutes we were both asleep.

I woke with the early dawn. The sun was just creeping up over the hills. Frank, still looking tense and worried, was still asleep. Poor Frank! Today I had to help him find a way to work things out. One thing I knew was that I would not leave without helping him.

Very quietly, I got out of the car and walked around a little. I looked at the land in the early morning, shimmering with the dawn. Australia always looked so beautiful in the early morning. Frank was sitting there looking at me as I returned to the car.

"I was very frightened when I woke up," Frank said. "I saw you were gone and was afraid that you had left during the night or that someone had kidnapped you."

"No," I said, laughing softly. "I'm here. I was just exploring."

"Are you staying with me?" he asked.

"Yes," I said slowly. "Today maybe you'd better think about going back. You don't want to spend your life running."

"Oh," he said, "we won't spend our lives running. Just a few days. Until we make some decent plans. I can't bear the thought of prison."

I said nothing, hoping to have another chance later that day to work on him.

He pulled out some bags from the back of the car. "We could make some coffee," he said. "I'll build a little fire." A little later we were drinking steaming coffee. I sat on a large rock by the side of the car, but Frank could not sit still. He drank his coffee while pacing back and forth.

As soon as I had finished my last drop, he gathered the stuff together. "Have a biscuit," he said, opening a bag. "But eat it in the car. We've got to get going. It's late already and we have a long way to go."

"Just where are we going?"

"We're headed south," he said, "down Coober Pedy way."

"Oh," I said, "the opal mines."

He winced. Then he said, "We'll have to skimp on food. I just can't stop at the rest stops. There are so few tourists that we'll be recognized."

I nodded, too sick at heart to say anything. I knew that the trip to Coober Pedy from the rock was long and lonely, over a dirt road.

Finally I said, "Please, Frank, let's be sensible. Before we take off on a road that very few travel we had better get food. We don't want to be another part of the legends of the deaths in the Great Outback of Australia."

Frank listened, then shrugged his shoulders. "I guess you're right," he said. "I see that I have to buy gas too."

We stopped at the next rest stop. A large sign at the entrance read: LAST STOP FOR 150 MILES.

"I'll get some food too," he said as I went to the restroom. "And please, Mellisa"—he looked at me with pleading eyes—"please do get back in the car. I need you."

I nodded again. What else could I do? When I got back in the car, the whole area seemed deserted. I guess Frank was negotiating for the groceries. Then I heard a voice from the back seat.

"Just relax, Melissa," it said. "I want to talk to old Frank when he returns."

I turned quickly, but I already knew who it was.

CHAPTER XXV

"Larry!" I exclaimed.

He looked at me, and I tried to read his eyes, but they told me nothing. I turned back to the front and waited for Frank.

Frank came slowly toward us. I knew that Larry was not visible from the front. I felt like a betrayer. But what could I do?

As soon as Frank got to the car, Larry sat up. "All right, Frank," he said. "Don't panic. Don't try to run away."

Frank looked pale. "Larry, please!"

Larry said, "Listen, Frank, you may not believe this, but I'm trying to help you. You've got to get this straightened out."

Frank drooped visibly. "There's no hope for me," he said slowly. "There's no hope."

"It's not that bad," said Larry.

"You don't know," said Frank. "You have no idea how I dread going to prison."

"Will it be worse than the prison of your own mind?"

181

Frank looked sadly at both of us. Then he turned to me. "I'm sorry, Melissa," he said. "I had hoped that somehow we could be together and you could help me cope with this. Larry's right."

"More than you think," said Larry. "Melissa has just broken out of her own prison."

"I—I," I stammered. How well Larry knew me!

"Well," Larry said, "come on, Frank. Let's go back to the rock."

Frank started the car and we headed back. Both men were silent, and I couldn't bear it.

Finally I burst out, "Now, please, will someone tell me the whole story?"

"I think you should, Larry," Frank said. "I think you owe it to her."

"Where to begin?" Larry mused.

"At the beginning."

"At the beginning," Larry said. "Well, I have to tell you something you don't know, Melissa. Frank and I could have been good friends. It was you who kept us apart."

"Me!"

"Yes," Frank said slowly, "we both were attracted to you. But now I know who won."

I turned and looked at Larry. This time I could read his eyes. They were full of love. I was stunned. A deep feeling of happiness filled me. And yet there were many unanswered questions.

"You two are so different," I said, "but you were both trying to do the same thing, catch Ralph Thompson. But Larry, what happened last night the first time at the aborigine compound?"

"That was another ploy. I pretended that I knew the satchel was in the compound. Ralph must have looked there before but I had been giving him a snow job of being an unusual detective. I wanted to force his hand. I even made a drawing in one of the caves pretending to point to the location."

"I saw it," I said.

"So did Ralph," Larry continued, "so that night I had to go there. I knew he would follow me. Naturally I found nothing. When he drew a gun on me, we talked about a deal. I told him that I knew it was stolen money and that I wanted a larger share of it. Of course, Ralph was furious. But he had been suspicious of me for a long time. I understood he even tried to make you leave me and the rock, thinking I might go too."

I was still puzzled. "But Larry," I said, "I heard a gunshot."

"Yes," said Larry, "before we made the deal, Ralph tried to prove that the gun was loaded, that he wasn't fooling. He shot the gun into the air."

"Did he also kill Colin?"

"I don't know," said Larry, "but it looks like it. Colin, with his photography, probably knew too much. And with Colin gone, the satchel may never be found. I didn't find it, nor did any of the people who were hired to. Ralph is now dead, Colin is dead, and Paul Morrison has been dead a long time. Maybe someday someone will find an old satchel buried in the ground here at the rock. But so far it's still wherever Paul put it."

"But Larry, you were in danger," I said. "Ralph could have killed you too."

"No," said Larry. "He was convinced that I knew where the satchel was. He was afraid to kill me until it was found. He had made that mistake once before."

"And later I killed Ralph," Frank said.

"It was an accident," I reminded him.

"You lost your head," Larry said.

"I lost my head over Melissa," said Frank.

I felt incomprehensible sorrow for Frank, but Larry had more to tell. "No," he said, "listen to me. There was a witness at the rock. Lynnette. She saw what happened. She'll testify for you."

"Lynnette." I repeated her name, waiting.

"Yes," Larry said. "There's a lot to say about the old girl. But suffice it to say that she was working with me."

"You were engaged to her," I said. "She wanted you back."

"We were once engaged," said Larry, "but I don't think she wants me back."

"But she told me to keep away from you."

"Yes," said Larry. "She told me she was going to do that. She told me that you loved me and that she could prove it. I'm glad she did."

The next few hours are a blur in my mind. But I remember the depth of feeling I felt for Larry, the way he looked at me with love.

And then there was the day when Larry and I again went to the rock. We stood there watching the setting sun, holding hands. It stood there, a huge mountain of strength, and Larry and I felt we belonged.